Sara Stewart graduated from the University of Newcastle-upon-Tyne with a BA in English and has worked in marketing and PR ever since, apart from the briefest of spells as a stand-up comedian. *Whilst I Was Out* is her first novel, but writing has always been at the heart of her career and she is a keen blogger. She has four cats of varying pedigrees, a tortoise, two hens and a rescue duck. Sara lives in the countryside where she loves walking slowly, whatever the weather.

Whilst I Was Out

Sara Stewart

Whilst I Was Out

Pegasus

PEGASUS PAPERBACK

ISBN- 978 1 910 90 303 2

*Pegasus is an imprint of
Pegasus Elliot MacKenzie Publishers Ltd.*
www.pegasuspublishers.com

First Published in 2016

**Pegasus
Sheraton House Castle Park
Cambridge CB3 0AX England**

Printed & Bound in Great Britain

To everyone, anywhere trapped in the wrong life.

INTRODUCTION

I have always been useless at meditation. So for me, yoga proved about as relaxing as a white-knuckle ride. There are several reasons for this, namely:

1/. My yoga mat making a farting noise when I landed my hefty weight upon it. Instead of ignoring this little incident, I felt obliged to explain to the entire class that the noise was not me breaking wind, but the yoga mat. Well, not the yoga mat breaking wind, but air inside being forced out through the tiniest of tears in the vinyl cover. I then demonstrated this again for the incredulous crowd. Everyone looked at me as if I was something nasty their young offspring had stepped in whilst on a posh 'play date'.

2/. Getting TOO relaxed during one particular session, only to wake myself up with a loud snort and discover I'd been drooling on the aforementioned mat. This resulted in a repeat performance of the 'face like a cat's arse' reaction from the yummy mummies of Richmond (upon Thames, of course).

3/. On the rare occasion I managed to stay with the instructor's spiel, she used the expression "far, far away". Those words did it for me. I mentally materialised as Princess Leia in the midst of some epic *Star Wars* battle. Not very relaxing at all.

Summoning up every ounce of self-control, I visually transported myself to a deserted tropical beach complete with clichéd swaying palms and azure blue waters. As for me, I was bronzed, toned and wearing a size nothing bikini with Cheryl Cole-confidence. And then from nowhere, appeared one of those irritating beach vendors who never take no for an answer. Not only did he cheekily invade my meditation, but also tried to sell me some god-awful friendship bracelet.

From then on I decided yoga was not for me and chose alcohol as my preferred method of chilling out.

So what in the great scheme of things does all this have to do with the tale in hand? In the words of a once-popular magician: "not a lot".

I was forty-two when I tried yoga and forty-two when I gave it up. Co-incidentally, the very same year my life began to unravel like a crocheted blanket.

It was morbidly fascinating. A bit like being transfixed by a car accident on the motorway even though you know you should look the other way. Like an observer, I watched my blanket of life disintegrate into chaotic balls of coloured wool without any obvious beginnings or endings.

CHAPTER 1

I should have realised my marriage was never going to work a long time before I decided to face the fact head on. Tell-tale signs such as being pinned to the wall by my throat or finding myself knocked to the ground when six months pregnant should all have been subtle give-aways. All courtesy of my dear husband, or MDH as he shall be known henceforth.

But it really started to dawn on me that something was seriously wrong the day MDH abandoned me in London, quite out of the blue.

We were stuck in the middle of rush hour traffic. He was driving, we were arguing. Just another normal day all told. Suddenly, he opened the driver's door, jumped out of the car and raced across Twickenham Green like something escaping from the Ape House at London Zoo.

For a moment, I sat open-mouthed at the surreal nature of what I had just witnessed, before a cacophony of car horns brought me back to reality. I shuffled awkwardly across from the passenger's seat, limply waved my apologies at the annoyed queue behind me and slowly drove home.

Four hours later, after I had made numerous frantic but fruitless phone calls, the doorbell rang and there was MDH sandwiched between two rather embarrassed-looking policemen. Apparently they had found him crouched behind a skip in a foetal position. Having delivered him to the front door, they awkwardly mumbled their goodbyes and that was that.

The second intimation we were knee-high in cow doo-doo took place on an average Sunday morning after the most desperate dinner party the previous evening. Although firmly entrenched in the 'Boden-catalogue-flowery-bunting' lifestyle, it didn't sit well with me. I wasn't the sort of mother who lingered outside the school gates at going-home time discussing the benefits of personal tennis coaching. I was disenamoured with the smug, perfectly manicured parents who carried the aroma of the day spa around with them. Apart from being too odd to be accepted within the clique, my perfume of choice was the local pub.

Anyway, back to dinner parties. I hated them. Attending was bad enough, but giving them was worse – the ultimate opportunity to be judged in the vulnerability of your own home.

Our guests that particular night were the parents of two young girls who were friendly with my three children. They had a veneer of pleasantness about them. It didn't help that MDH was obsessed with the wife thanks to her "Agnetha-from-Abba" good looks and the fact she was something god-like in marketing. Her husband, an orthopaedic surgeon, had a strange connection to Princess Diana's post-mortem that I could never quite fathom out.

At the time, I was going through one of my many attempts at abstinence. I didn't drink a thing all evening and had to watch the other three neck down several bottles of red wine. MDH and 'the other woman' flirted outrageously using innuendoes that would have had the *Carry On* brigade blushing.

MDH also went in for one of his favourite past-times – wife baiting – putting in an Olympic-standard performance that evening. He managed to cover a host of disciplines – my cooking, my fashion sense and my smoking. It was one of those nights when I desperately wanted the floor to open up and swallow me whole.

So, when MDH asked me the next morning whether I still loved him, as I was serving up a cooked breakfast that looked as badly burnt as my pride felt, I truthfully answered that I wasn't certain. It triggered a rather extraordinary response.

He sat bolt upright at the table and became as stiff as a board. His face turned bright red and he began to make a noise like a bumblebee at a rave. He then keeled over onto the floor with a loud, buzzing sound still issuing forth.

My kids were a little startled, to say the least. At the time, they were all aged under ten. It was a bizarre sight, even for me, so they must have felt their world was slowly crashing in around them (which, sadly to say, it was just about to). I ushered them upstairs, trying to divert them with the giant Playmobil castle I'd just bought them, courtesy of a vast toy town mortgage.

Back in the kitchen, MDH's fit seemed to be coming to an end. As per his previous odd turns, he stood up without saying a word and disappeared down to The Shed at the bottom of the garden. The Shed was a dark and evil place where normal human beings were forbidden to enter. It was filled with skeletal bike frames, rotting magazines and gadgets for just about everything – most of which were still pristine and in their packaging.

MDH was obsessed with cycling and spent most of his time – and my money – on his hobby. To this day, I find it hard to pass a Lycra-clad cyclist on the road without a desperate urge to nudge them into the ditch. Although I manage to resist, I still hiss at them as you do the evil antagonist in a pantomime.

Cycling ruled all of our lives. Having returned home after giving birth to my daughter – our second child – I was left on my own for the weekend with a new baby and our eighteen-month-old son. MDH had decided to head off to Flanders with a similarly ridiculously Spandex-clad mate to bob eagerly along in the wake of some bloody bike race.

He would cycle to work, train on his bike most evenings before coming home, insist on riding at least a hundred miles on a Saturday as well as competing in a race nearly every Sunday. I remember standing at the sink most Saturday mornings, tears streaming down my face as I faced the prospect of another grim weekend. I was at my wits' end trying to cope with three small children all by myself, having worked my proverbial nuts off during the week.

I started to loathe the sight of him in his head-to-toe cycling gear. He reminded me of a bit-part performer from the Cirque Du Soleil complete with a stupid, pointy helmet that was meant to assist with aerodynamics. He also made free with my razor to shave off every inch of his body hair in the name of streamlining.

The clickety-clack sound made by the metal cleats of his cycling shoes had me grinding my teeth with intense irritation as they left little pockmarks across my stripped wood floors.

Then there was the endless array of dripping black bib-shorts hanging from the bathroom shower that depressed the hell out of me. At bedtimes, a little light reading of *Cycling Weekly* was in order for MDH – I was convinced he'd rather masturbate looking at an advertisement for handlebar tape than the centrefold of *Playboy*.

And it was cycling that led me to make the decision, which resulted in our domestic 9/11.

***

MDH and I ran a business together – or should I say, he ran it and I was forced to go along with his disastrous decisions and leadership style.

At one time, our agency had been hot property with a client list to turn *Campaign* readers green with envy. Like everything else in our lives, it was now as toxic as someone going through chemo. Both clients and staff were abandoning us like hair leaving a cancer patient's head.

Running your own business is tough so whenever I got pregnant, I worked right up to the point of giving birth. MDH explained to me, all very logically, that the business simply couldn't afford for me to take any time off. As it was, hospital visits, afternoon naps and suchlike would mean I'd be away from the office a little too often for his liking.

The morning my daughter was born, I was at work and in the process of making coffee for everyone. I was having a few twinges but didn't think they were that significant.

Anyway, a couple of hours later, I was on my back at Queen Charlotte's Hospital cresting the waves of contractions and pushing out my little girl like choux pastry from an icing bag. The next day, I was back at my computer trying to breastfeed and deal with clients on the phone, all at the same time. At night, I would have recurring dreams that I was in the middle of a meeting when my boobs started self-expressing like some odd cartoon breast fountains.

I didn't take a single day's maternity leave after giving birth. All three of my kids were packed off to nursery at just three months old, having been looked after by a maternity nurse prior to that. The guilt I went through meant I often turned to the bottle to self-medicate. Except mine was filled with alcohol, and not formula.

So when MDH announced he'd decided to take a sabbatical to get his head straight, I was completely gobsmacked. This soon turned to anger when I discovered his plan was to head off for a month to follow the Tour De France on his blasted bicycle. MDH had finally gone completely bonkers.

The business was at the point where a priest should have been called in to deliver the last rites. I was downing a couple of bottles of Baileys each evening and we were going through nannies faster than you could say Von Trapp.

The madness just escalated. For weeks prior to his French leave, MDH practised his camping techniques in our suburban back garden in full view of all the neighbours. What made it worse was the fact he wasn't even using a tent. He had pitched some military poncho in the shrubbery, almost as if he was on some SAS mission.

Being ex-Services, everything for the trip had to be done with ridiculous precision. MDH bought a bike trailer to cart all his gear across France together with some Heath Robinson contraption to secure everything in place. He accumulated things that folded down to a hundredth of their size and gadgets that could do things like turning a kettle into a shower. I pointed out that he was cycling across France not exploring unchartered territory in deepest Peru.

I noticed his supplies also included an industrial-size pack of condoms. When I challenged him, I was foolish enough to fall for his story. According to MDH, condoms were standard Forces issue and used for all sorts of military emergencies. He demonstrated by showing me how useful a condom could be for carrying water. My mind boggled.

MILITARY EMERGENCIES WHERE CONDOMS MIGHT PROVE USEFUL

1/. Lack of armaments emergency – fill condom with liquid, tie a knot and throw forcibly at enemy

2/. Surprise alien attack emergency – pull condom over head, inflate with own breath, disguise yourself as an alien and merge with a passing group

3/. Soggy footwear emergency – use two condoms as make-do waterproof socks

4/. Lack of party decorations emergency – blow up several condoms, knot and tie a string to each

Anyway, the day of MDH's departure to France arrived. One of the guys from work volunteered to drive him down to Portsmouth to catch the ferry. Why he couldn't cycle there himself as a warm-up for his adventure was beyond me? But by this stage, I wanted to distance myself from the whole pitiful performance. Despite the stress I was going to be under trying to juggle everything whilst he was away, it was a blessed relief to see his bottom bracket disappear into l'horizon.

"Peace," I sighed. "Peace for an entire month."

How wrong could I have been?

Within hours of crossing the channel, the Tour De France had turned into the Tour De Farce. Each day brought a new disaster, which necessitated endless phone calls from MDH to update everyone on his lack of progress.

For a start, the sheer weight of all his irritating little accessories had caused both the bike and the trailer to buckle. Not only did he have to ditch a lot of stuff in some left-luggage locker (which remains in some nameless French station to this day), but MDH also had to use most of his spending money on repairs. More bloody expense!

As his luck would have it, France experienced its worst summer flooding for centuries. Even the sturdiest of tents wouldn't have held back the ebb and flow of angry waters so a camping poncho didn't stand a chance. It disappeared down the Loire as fast as you could say *couteau*.

17

MDH claimed that sleeping in foul water had resulted in a nasty bout of dysentery, which had brought on a terrible outcrop of haemorrhoids. Not ideal when you're planning to spend weeks perched on a saddle as sharp as a razor and designed for professional cyclists (they must have cast-iron bottoms, that's all I can say). Not a lot I could do to help from the other side of the Channel and "no, I didn't know the French word for pile cream".

His behaviour became increasingly erratic and I was on the receiving end of most of it. MDH would send me a daily photo of himself via his mobile. Other than charting the growth of his designer stubble, I couldn't see a point to it. Perhaps there wasn't one. However, the relentless daily presence of MDH's expressionless face and haunted eyes had me knocking back the drink soon after breakfast.

Just after I'd finished the daily staff briefing, MDH would ring in and counter each and every decision I'd made. If anyone dared to challenge him, he would rant down the phone until they were a gibbering wreck.

In addition to the daily barrage of calls, MDH got hold of me every night after imbibing in some bar tabac, timed to catch me just as I was nodding off. If I switched off my mobile, he'd call the landline barking message after message each time the answering machine kicked in.

MDH eventually caught up with the Tour De France somewhere in Provence. That said, his attention seemed to be more focussed on a woman he had met at some eco campsite. Although she was staying there with her husband, MDH taunted me daily with details of their starlit trysts. No doubt acting out some military emergency with the industrial-size pack of condoms.

The saddest thing was, I didn't have the energy to muster up the merest hint of jealousy. Instead I took myself off to the pub most lunchtimes for several sneaky G&Ts. Before going back to the office, I stocked up on enough alcohol to see me through the next twenty-four hours.

MDH's month-long cycling escapade somehow extended to six weeks. I was now drinking at work and doing a poor job of hiding this from my staff. I think I began to scare the majority of the team who, until that point, had blamed MDH for all the problems the business was having.

MDH eventually made it back to good old Blighty. I agreed to pick him up from the ferry. As he cycled off the boat, I became aware that he'd completely shaved his head, was sporting henna tattoos on his forearms and was wearing an array of strange, hippy-like jewellery. No doubt love tokens from 'eco-campsite girl'.

We went for a coffee and MDH made a great display of showing me a brand new Rolex he'd bought himself from duty free. No gifts were forthcoming for either me or the kids. Not even so much as a thank you for any of my input at work or at home, allowing him the time to go and sort his even balder head out.

As we paid for our drinks, he announced loudly and much to the surprise of everyone in Starbucks that he'd spent the two-day ferry crossing locked in his cabin manicuring his toenails. He wanted to complete his embodiment of physical perfection. I nearly threw up in my venti wet latte!

Enough of this madness. In the process of sorting his own head out, he'd done mine in. Something had to change.

CHAPTER 2

A mere thirty minutes after the return of MDH from his Grand Tour, I decided it was time to dump my marriage in the recycle bin. Had I not been anaesthetised most of the time with booze, I would have done the sensible thing and asked for a divorce before heading off to create a sane new life for myself, and the kids. But this option never crossed my mind. I wasn't capable of rational thought and to make the break, I needed a safe haven to stagger to. My solution was to have an affair.

When I was a child, I'd always been more interested in playing games of sexual discovery with little girls rather than little boys. Instead of 'Doctors and Nurses', I much preferred 'Nurses and Nurses'. Similarly, when a boy suggested a round of 'I'll show you mine if you show me yours', I hadn't the slightest interest in discovering what he kept in his Brentford Nylon Y-fronts. I'd turn tail and run, seeking refuge in the arms of the latest teacher I'd developed a massive crush on. Female of course.

Whilst my friends were 'getting it on' at the village hall disco with the local grammar school boys, I found myself more interested in hanging out with their older sisters. I'd happily spend hours over a Cherry B swopping make-up tips from *Jackie* magazine with them.

Eventually, in a bid to conform, I forced myself to start fancying the opposite sex but discovered they had to be twice my age to provide any sort of frisson. I'm sure Freud would have had a field day!

I lost my fifteen-year-old virginity to a thirty-two-year-old martial arts instructor during a window of opportunity between Saturday morning judo lessons at the church hall. And so began my lacklustre approach to sex with men, which seemed to be something you fitted in between washing up and the ironing and about as appealing as household chores.

Despite my best efforts, I continued to find myself in tepid relationships throughout my student years and into early adulthood. So I was stunned to find myself head-over-heels in love for the first time (or so I thought) whilst on a skiing holiday in Austria. And even more astonished that the object of my affections was a diminutive middle-aged woman, old enough to be my mother.

Talking of which, I was keen to secure the blessing of my mother regarding the recent about turn in my sexual preferences. Off I went to spend the weekend with my parents, filled with excitement about sharing my good news. I opted to tell her when we were making up my bed, tentatively sounding her out on the subject of Sapphic love.

When she spewed the words 'perverted, sick, unnatural and damned to hell', I realised I wasn't batting for the winning side. She swiftly changed the subject to that of grandchildren and how she couldn't wait until she had some. As an only child, this was a clear message to stick to the heterosexual path on which she thought I should be headed. With a final plump of the pillows, she turned on her heel and left.

I gave up any gay attempts and made the calamitous decision to be a dutiful daughter. After wandering about in the wilderness of love for several more years, I tripped over MDH. He had been my diving instructor and I'd always had a bit of thing for rubber!

***

21

So I decided that the time had come to find out whether the nagging doubts I'd had about my sexuality were for real. Not only did I need to have an affair, but it also had to be with a woman. In for a penny, in for a Penny.

But how do you go about finding a gay lover in your forties? Especially one who would happily take on board a married woman with "no previous experience" and three small children? Having no idea about 'the scene', the prospect of hanging around in some gay bar on the off-chance of getting lucky didn't really appeal to me. Besides, I didn't trust myself not to get totally blotto and make a complete arse of myself.

How to make a complete arse of yourself

You will need:

* *One crowded karaoke bar in a small French seaside resort*
* *A pitcher of margaritas*
* *One six-year-old daughter*
* *Britney Spears's (Hit Me)*Baby One More Time *on your karaoke request list*

Method

- *Drink the pitcher of margaritas all by yourself and as fast as you can.*
- *Put in a request to sing Britney Spears's* (Hit Me) Baby One More Time *at said karaoke bar.*
- *When your turn is announced, stagger up to the stage, daughter in one hand, lit cigarette in the other.*

- *Begin slurred rendition of Britney complete with dance movements.*
- *Turn to smile conspiratorially at daughter only to discover she's legged it in embarrassment.*
- *Add insult to injury by realising the bar staff have switched off the microphone because your pissed Britney rendition isn't entertaining ANY ONE.*
- *Extinguish your cigarette in someone's drink on your way back to the table where each member of your family is sitting in complete, red-faced silence.*
- *Leave bar immediately and avoid visiting it again for the duration of the holiday.*

The SoulMates' pages of *The Guardian* came to my rescue. Here the Holy Grail of womanhood was surely to be found – my knightress in see-through armour. Having nervously scanned the Women Seeking Women section, I decided four of them sounded vaguely suitable – not bad going out of a total of six small ads, I suppose.

The system worked like this. You dialled the allocated number printed next to your 'chosen one' and listened to the message they'd recorded about themselves. If they sounded slightly human, you could leave a response together with your personal contact details.

Having listened to the messages, my four were quickly whittled down to two. One had such as thick Scouse accent I couldn't understand a word and the other sounded on the verge of suicide. I'd had my fill of manic depressives for the time being. So I left two rather faltering and scatty messages for the remaining ladies and threw myself at the mercy of the goddesses.

Woman No. 1 was the first to ring me just a day later. She was delightful and also happened to live in France – my favourite place on the planet, despite MDH's best efforts to sully it for me. It wasn't long before the initial excitement wore off. The practicalities of popping down to the Dordogne for a 'quickie' seemed somewhat extreme. Despite being a virtuoso when it came to deceit, even I would struggle to find reasons to head off to France a couple of times a month.

Lying, you see, is an absolute must for the practising alcoholic e.g. "no, of course I haven't been drinking, that's mouthwash you can smell" and "no, of course I don't normally keep a selection of miniatures in my glove compartment, a friend gave them to me to look after".

So, with a heavy heart, I had to say no to my first potential amoureuse.

A couple of days elapsed and I got a text message from Woman No. 2 who was called Anna. Instead of ringing, her opening gambit was to send a text with her email address. I thought this was a really thoughtful way to introduce herself and later that evening I nervously sent my first gay email.

Anna was quick to respond and within the hour, emails had pinged back and forth covering meaningful topics such as *Coronation Street*, *EastEnders* and *Emmerdale*.

I had not begun as honestly as I should with my new lady love – explaining that my husband had died tragically in some 'military emergency' (exploding industrial-sized condoms, no doubt). I was a lonely widow struggling to bring up three children. In one email to Anna, I joked that I sounded like some sad creature from a Dickens' novel. Who's Dickens, came the reply and it wasn't sent with any intended irony?

I was immediately distracted from my literary disappointment by the photo she sent of herself. She was gorgeous. No dungarees, no Doc Martens and no facial piercings. Anna was the archetypal lipstick lesbian. I was already in lust, intoxicated with the heady prospect of my first real sexual experience with a woman. I hadn't felt like this since my brief encounter with that pair of menopausal lips all those years ago in the Alps.

Over the next couple of weeks, whilst we continued to email and text voraciously, I couldn't get up the courage to talk to her on the phone. I didn't want to make a fool of myself and neither did I want this vision of loveliness to disappoint me. I knew we couldn't carry on like this forever, but unlike most blokes would have been, Anna was patient and understanding. It made me fall even harder for her.

Things reached bursting point when I went away for the weekend with MDH. I had booked and paid for a couple of days away in Brittany months ago. The prospect of spending time cocooned in a small fishing village with him filled me with despair, but there was no escaping it. At least Anna could come with me, albeit virtually and courtesy of my mobile.

MDH didn't seem to notice that I was texting like a teenager even before we left the outskirts of London – slightly odd since I'd only learnt this communication skill since Anna had come on the scene. As for Anna, I'd told her my best mate was taking me away for the weekend to give me a break from the kids.

For forty-eight hours over crepes, mussels and huge amounts of Calvados, a flurry of passionate and frustrated love texts made their way back and forth across the Channel.

At some point during the weekend, I decided I wanted additional content over and above the 'XXX's or the 'I want U's. I was aching to discover more about her as a person and the things that interested her.

I sent a series of questions:

What is your favourite film of all time and what did you last see at the cinema?
No response.
What are your political views?
No response.
Are you religious or spiritual?
Still no response.

Anna went completely silent on me for several hours. I started to panic. I scrutinised every text I had sent to establish whether I'd written anything offensive or that could have been misinterpreted. There was nothing I could find. Perhaps she'd been involved in an accident. Just my luck for everything to come to a tragic end before it had even begun. Paranoia set in.

A few hours later, she sent a text saying she'd been out shopping and had forgotten her mobile. This struck me as odd given her phone had been joined to her at the hip these past few weeks. I never got any answers to my more probing questions and the stream of 'sweetie, honey' pleasantries ensued. I was so relieved to have re-established contact, I'd have been happy if she'd sent me her grocery list.

It was only later that I discovered Anna hadn't read a book since leaving school. It wasn't that she was unable to read books or didn't have the intellect to understand them. She simply wasn't curious about things and hadn't really the patience either. She didn't see the point! Neither had she any political views or ever considered the concept of spirituality. The truth being, if things didn't have a direct or immediate impact on her life, she wasn't interested.

Now the thing is, if I had known about sociopaths or stopped to listen to those people who had tried to warn me, these sorts of details would have been the start of an entire United Nations' worth of red flags being waved in front of me. What's more, they would have been embroidered with words like 'stop' 'proceed no further' 'danger ahead'.

But I hadn't heard of sociopaths and I hadn't the time for good advice, so I tuned out the distant voices in my 'sensible head' that whispered something was wrong.

CHAPTER 3

There was no way to postpone speaking to Anna any longer. The weekend in France had pushed the pair of us to a near fever pitch of desire. Continuing our relationship on this virtual level would have driven me insane.

Driving home from work the following week, I found a beautiful spot to pull over in Richmond Park, summoned all my courage and tentatively called her mobile. She answered immediately. Her voice was the most beguiling I had ever heard – like warm chocolate slowly being poured all over you. Anna could have easily been one of those continuity women on Radio 4.

'So, you're finally ready to do the talking thing eh?' she teased gently.

'Err, yes,' I replied eloquently.

We'd long discussed via email when we should do the "talking thing".

My heart was pounding and felt like it was stuck in my throat. But I soon overcame my nerves thanks to Anna's constant stream of flattery and the attention she lavished upon me. She still remained reticent when it came to divulging specifics about her thoughts on the meaning of life. However, I discovered we drove the same make of car, both had our motorbike license and she was currently wearing a camel-coloured suit and high heels teamed with black underwear. My downstairs' department did an immediate leapfrog.

Anna also informed me she lived in a beautiful old stone house in a picturesque East Midlands village.

Ah, the romantic East Midlands. A place that had previously seemed little more than a world of coal mines and shoe factories now took on a utopian brilliance.

Despite being desperate to get together, it was now Anna who had plans that were going to get in our way. She had promised to attend some gay woman's sixtieth birthday celebrations the coming weekend. Apparently the woman was a former girlfriend of hers, but there was going to be a crowd of people staying at the house and their relationship had ended a long time ago. Over time, I was to discover most of the women that littered Anna's past had, at some stage, littered her bed too.

There was nothing for me to worry about, she cooed. Strangely, the thought of impropriety hadn't even crossed my mind. I felt completely certain that I was Anna's sole focus. Besides, I could hardly justify being jealous given I was living with MDH who she still believed had been buried with full military honours.

We agreed to meet one evening the following week. The location we chose was a rather chichi boutique hotel halfway between London and Nottingham. I was beside myself with anticipation. I immediately began to prepare myself for the date, which I prayed, would change my life forever. Oh to be released from my current domestic misery.

Ever since 'meeting' Anna, I'd stopped drinking and smoking – again. I hadn't wanted to let myself down by sending any drunken, inappropriate emails or by ringing her up whilst half cut. I was convinced I could remain on the straight and narrow for this woman. Well, the narrow at least.

I spent the next couple of days scouring the shops for the perfect outfit. I knew Anna loved feminine women so I bought the girliest ensemble I could find. A diaphanous pink silk floral skirt with a matching T-shirt and a cardigan edged with flourishes of ribbons. It wasn't really me. Don't get me wrong, I love skirts, dresses, jewellery, make-up etc., but too many added extras on clothing make me nervous. I once saw someone get his overly large anorak toggles (not a euphemism, I hasten to add) caught in a pair of lift doors as they were closing. The ensuing vignette put me right off clothing fripperies.

A pair of ridiculously high heels completed the look and all that was left to do was primp and preen myself. I undertook this task with health spa professionalism – I kept leave-in conditioner in my hair for the next five days, despite some strange looks from my colleagues. I exfoliated myself to the point of self-abuse and removed virtually every hair on my body with an exuberant application of Immac. I had the air of a prepubescent chicken.

Date-Day finally arrived. I had told MDH that I was meeting an old friend who was having boyfriend trouble and to expect me home late – very late. To avoid any cause for suspicion, I stopped at a pub en route to change into my little pink number and nervously apply excessive amounts of make-up.

As I pulled in to the hotel car park, I could see Anna's Audi convertible already parked up. I pulled into the space next to hers, as she had instructed me to do. With one final application of lip gloss, I got out of the car and with my heart almost audibly pounding, teetered across the drive.

I had to make my way through a warren of rooms to reach the bar, which seemed to take an eternity in my stupid shoes.

When I arrived at my final destination, my heart was racing so fast I felt I was going to faint. All those weeks of anticipation and there she was.

My heart plummeted to the lowest point of my stilettoes. It was the strangest sensation I'd ever experienced. Despite having seen numerous photos of her, the woman sitting across the room didn't match my mental image of Anna. Not in the slightest.

The voice was Anna's all right, but it was emanating from the body of a stranger. It was a bit creepy. Instead of eyebrows, she'd had a pair of lines tattooed in their place. It gave her a look of permanent surprise. Her spiked hair reminded me of the '80s' singer Howard Jones. Sadly, I'd never been a fan. What's more, it was so unbelievably thin I could see right through to her scalp like one of those old dolls you see lying around at a charity shop.

Realising I was standing there open-mouthed, I tried to look for the positives. Her dress sense was immaculate. She wore a crisp white shirt tucked into tight black jeans together with a pair of highly covetable boots. She had a fantastic figure without a spare inch of fat and she certainly didn't look anywhere close to her fifty years. Must have made a pact with the Devil, I remember thinking to myself.

Her comfortably-casual look made me feel hideously overdressed and I immediately apologised for being so 'done up'. I made up the excuse/lie that I'd come straight from press day at Chelsea Flower Show, hence the floral garb.

All I wanted to do was turn tail and run, but given I had invested so much emotionally in the potential of this relationship I decided to try to get beyond her Aunt Sally exterior.

Anna had bought all sorts of things with her to show me, such as a menu from her favourite restaurant and leaflets about the area where she lived. I felt like I was meeting a tourist attraction and not a potential lover. I couldn't understand why she needed this stuff to define who she was.

I was also finding it impossible to relax because of my ridiculous outfit so I decided I to go and change. I made my excuses and headed back to the car.

In a moment of complete clarity, I knew the best thing to do would be to get in my car, drive back to London and put all this nonsense behind me. I could ring Anna on the way home, apologise and tell her it had all been a terrible mistake. I decided to call MDH and declare my love for him. More than anything I wanted to speak to my kids. Suddenly I felt so lonely.

Perhaps if he'd answered, I would have stuck to plan B. Instead, I got his morose, monotone voicemail message and suddenly Anna seemed the lesser of two evils.

I returned wearing the more casual clothes I'd had on all day.

'Let's get out of here,' she suggested when I'd just settled back into my seat. 'It's all a little too formal – I'd prefer a country pub if that's all right with you?"

I agreed although I was desperate for a drink after the long drive. Anna offered to take me in her car and I happily went along with the plan. Had it been a first date with a man, I'd have insisted on following in my own car. I thought it was highly unlikely that Anna was going to force herself upon me or take me hostage. I felt completely safe.

My non-smoking resolve melted and I asked Anna to stop at a garage so I could buy some cigarettes. She leapt out of the car and bought me a packet of Richmond Menthol, her favourite brand, despite the fact I'd asked for Silk Cut. I was gushingly appreciative.

As soon as we walked into the pub, I knew I was going to have to knock back a drink to further calm my nerves. I ordered a G&T.

Shortly after we'd settled at a table with our drinks, I realised it was my children's bedtime so I gave them a quick ring to say goodnight. Normally I was there to put them to bed and I felt really terrible. I was delighted to see Anna smiling at me as I chatted to them. When I'd finished the call, she told me how much she liked kids and regretted never having had any herself. She added how much more attractive she found women with children.

She went on to tell me that her last 'real' relationship had also been with a married woman who'd had two young children and no previous same-sex experience. The woman in question left her family to move in with Anna but after a year or so, it hadn't worked out and Anna had ended it. Apparently, the woman was too much of a home-bird and not ambitious enough for Anna.

Here was the biggest red flag so far. So big, I should have felt its strong breeze waft in my face. A pattern as a serial home-wrecker was emerging in front of me. Either I didn't see it or subconsciously I chose to ignore it. The only thing I took away from this little exchange was the fact Anna loved children. I seemed to have found the perfect person with whom to create the dream family I had always wanted.

After a second G&T and a couple of cigarettes, I now thought Anna was a real looker. In days to come, people would point out that her strange eyebrows made her look like a scary Ronald McDonald. I would leap to her defence immediately. I never thought of her as odd-looking again.

With unusual self-restraint, I managed to limit myself to just two drinks that evening. As I paid the bar bill, Anna went ahead to warm up the car as the night had suddenly turned chilly. As I climbed into the passenger seat, I noticed Anna was staring at me intently. Her pupils were so dilated the thought she might be on drugs crossed my mind.

Like a slow-motion scene from a film, she pulled me towards her and gently kissed me. I cannot describe how unbelievable that first kiss proved to be. Her lips were delicate and soft. Her skin felt like velvet against mine. There was no comparison to kissing MDH or any man I had ever known. It was sensual, tender, erotic and warm and left me craving for more.

Anna pulled away from me with a slight smile.

"Shall we find somewhere a little more private?"

I found myself nodding back at her like some village idiot. My power of speech seemed to have vanished. My heart was fluttering and I experienced a sense of longing that I'd never known before. My entire body was tingling – I felt alive and incredibly turned on. Nothing had ever seemed as erotic as this.

Anna found a secluded back lane and pulled the car over, drawing me towards her as soon as we stopped. She pushed herself into me more urgently this time and I caught a hint of Immac. I was reminded of the fact I was being intimate with a woman. How the essence of hair removal cream can intensify a moment of passion, I have no idea. But it did.

She gently moved her hand under my T-shirt and stroked my skin, careful to avoid touching my breasts. We continued to kiss for another hour without going any further. For that very reason it was one of the most sensual experiences I'd ever known. She had an amazing repertoire with her mouth and tongue. The best foreplay I had experienced.

Reluctantly, I drew away from her. It was well past midnight and both of us had over an hour's drive ahead. Had she suggested getting a room in the chichi boutique hotel there and then, I would have leapt at the chance. My desire to be completely naked and roll around in bed with her was desperate.

Anna drove us silently back to the hotel car park and we shared one last kiss.

"Will I see you again?" she asked quietly.

"Of course," I replied.

All the reservations from earlier had evaporated. I had fallen head over heels in love with this woman and the thought of never seeing her again was terrifying.

"I'll call you then, darling," she said. As I got out of the car, she tenderly squeezed my hand instead of saying goodbye.

Driving off, I noticed Anna watching me through her driver's window. It struck me how large her eyes looked and how much of the whites I could see beneath her irises. I remember my mother telling me that you couldn't trust people with eyes like that. Poached egg eyes, she called them. I laughed it off. My mother had also warned me against men in white socks. Come to think of it, didn't MDH wear white socks?

My overwhelming impression was how incredibly sad Anna looked and it broke my heart to leave her.

We hadn't made any specific plans for getting together again, but it didn't bother me. I knew we would arrange something as soon as we could.

Little did I know that the fickle finger of fate would ensure we'd see each other again in just a couple of days.

She rang me on the drive home to tell me that she was "crazily in love" with me. I was the one she'd been waiting for all her life and she wanted to spend the rest of her days with me. I was desperate to believe her. I wanted this to be my fairy-tale ending and I echoed all her sentiments.

When I got home MDH's evening debris lay scattered about the place. A couple of empty beer cans had been abandoned where they'd been guzzled. A plate, with a half-eaten pizza and a PlayStation controller perched on it, had been left in the middle of the floor. *Medal of Honour* still crackled on the TV screen.

I made my way upstairs and went to tuck in my sleeping children. They looked so innocent and vulnerable. I began to chastise myself about missing their bedtime, justifying it by saying it was a necessary part of the process in creating a new life for us all. Silently I kissed each of them on their forehead.

As I tiptoed into the bedroom, MDH's snores greeted me. Clasped to his chest was the obligatory copy of *Cycling Weekly*. He didn't stir as I got into bed. I slipped under the covers at great pains to avoid any physical contact with him whatsoever.

MDH had once said to me that all I needed was a bobble hat to complete my night-time 'there's no way I'm having sex with you' look. How right he was. Being approached by an erect penis put me in mind of being pierced by an unsavoury little cocktail sausage. I couldn't stand the piggy sex faces men pulled as they sweated away on top of you.

I was never to make love with a man again.

CHAPTER 4

I woke up full of the joys of spring – well, the joys of Anna actually. I felt like I was walking on air. Whenever I thought about her, I got a jolt in my heart as if I'd just been defibrillated. This was accompanied by a melting sensation in my stomach. There was no doubt about it. I had fallen for Anna in a big way.

MDH had farted his way out of bed before heading off for a spinning class at the local gym. I always imagined him sitting like Rumpelstiltskin rustling up rubber yarn from disused inner tubes. But, of course, it was another form of exercise involving a bicycle. As he left, he'd grunted in monosyllables that he had decided to work from home today.

Excellent. The office would be tension free and I could enjoy my new-found happiness without reprisal.

Even the congestion on the way to work didn't bother me as I was in such a good mood. I let people pull out ahead of me and there was none of my usual knob-head gestures to any drivers who irritated me. A soppy text from Anna added to my ecstasy.

I spent the morning working, punctuated by silly emails to Anna and drooling over an assortment of new photos of herself she'd sent me. I was happy, happy, happy. But, elation always comes before a fall.

Suddenly my computer seemed to take on a mind of its own. Folders opened by themselves. The cursor seemed possessed. All I could do was watch open-mouthed. And then the horrible truth hit me. Someone had accessed my computer remotely.

My mobile rang. It was MDH.

"Come home. We need to talk. I know all about Anna."

Devious little shit! He had been rootling around my Mac and had read every email that had ever passed between Anna and myself. I was up to my ears in the deepest of shit.

Unlike my earlier idyllic drive to work, the journey home felt like I was making my way to the guillotine. There was no point in denying anything to MDH as he had uncovered all the evidence, but I had no idea what to say. I just went into autopilot for the rest of the day.

We'd agreed to meet at a local watering hole rather than at home to avoid our nanny *de jour* overhearing the heated exchange that would no doubt ensue.

As I arrived, I spotted MDH already installed in pole position outside the bar, a pint in one hand and a virtual club in the other. His face was grey and his eyes were more dead fish-like than ever. I ordered myself a double vodka and ginger beer – I deserved a Moscow Mule with the kicking I was about to get.

"I want you to ring this woman right now and tell her it's over," was MDH's opening gambit. Even before I'd had the chance to sit down, he thrust his mobile at me.

I answered without even thinking.

"No, I am not going to give her up. She makes me happy."

"You get on that phone now and speak to her. You are NOT gay and you don't know the meaning of the word 'happy'."

"You're not going to bully me any longer. I love Anna." Good God, where had that come from?

He rolled his eyes skyward and grinned sarcastically.

"You found this woman in the small ads, you've met her once and you claim to be in love? Don't be ridiculous."

"Ridiculous or not, it's how I feel and I know she feels the same way about me. Our marriage is over and you're going to have to deal with it."

I could feel alcohol-induced confidence taking hold. With his jaw set, I watched MDH calmly dial a number. My first thought was that he was calling Anna. When he started speaking, I realised he was talking to my mother, informing her I had decided to become a lesbian and was now involved with a woman. Oh well, she couldn't complain about not having grandchildren – she had three of them now.

He then made a second call, this time to his father and went through exactly the same exercise. All I could do was sit there with a bemused look on my face. What next? Perhaps the headmaster of the children's school or one of the spinning instructors at the gym would like to know about my personal life, I suggested?

We spent the rest of the day going round in circles accompanied by various alcoholic beverages. I felt terribly anxious, but for all the wrong reasons. I could see texts from Anna mounting up on my mobile as she tried to make contact.

Our one-sided conversation continued along the same lines for five hours – "leave her", "if you don't leave her our world will fall apart", "you're not having the kids if you leave", "you'll get no money from the business" and so on. To be honest, anaesthetised with vodka and still glowing from the previous night, I didn't care about anything except:

1/ talking to Anna

2/ getting home in time to see the kids before they went to bed

Eventually MDH angrily pushed the table away from him and stomped off. I looked at my watch. It was time for his evening bike ride. Even teetering on the very edge of his personal precipice, dressing up in

Lycra and pounding his quadriceps took priority. I stayed to finish my drink.

I staggered home wearily. MDH was right in a way. I hardly knew this woman. Would I be able to count on her in my hour of need, given I hadn't been totally honest with her about my marital situation. Lies had a horrible way of rearing their ugly little heads and giving you a sharp bite in the arse.

As I sat watching a 'show' my children had devised for me, my head was whirling dervishly as I tried to decide on the best course of action.

Later that evening, MDH returned from his ride red-faced and in a foul mood. You could always measure the severity of his temper by the depth of the cleat marks he left in the floor. That night they would have been deep enough for a nice mix of bedding plants.

Negotiations recommenced once the kids were in bed. This time he was not going to take no for an answer and demanded that I speak to Anna. His latest brainwave was for the three of us to get together the following evening to discuss our collective futures.

Having seen a similar look in his eyes many times before, I knew I had no choice but to make the call if I wanted to avoid a beating. Weirdly, the thought of telling Anna that I was not a widow and still living with my very-much-alive husband worried me more than a possible thick lip. My stomach began to do the rumba. I was certain she would end it, there and then.

I got out my mobile and nervously dialled her number whilst MDH breathed down my neck. Anna answered almost immediately, sounding flustered:

"Darling, where have you been? I've been texting you all day? Is everything OK?"

Before I had time to utter a word, MDH had snatched the phone out of my hand and delivered his little speech, which no doubt he had been practising to the turn of his tyres earlier that evening.

"Anna, you don't know me but let me introduce myself. I'm your new girlfriend's husband. I gather you are having an affair with my wife although I appreciate you, too, have been misled and believe I am dead? Now you are aware of my existence, let me hand you back to Alice."

My hand was shaking as I took the phone and croaked out a pitiful hello.

"Is this true?" she asked.

"Yes I'm afraid it is, but that doesn't change the way I feel about you. I thought you wouldn't be interested in a married woman with all the complications it entailed. I am so sorry."

A moment or two passed and then she spoke:

"I need some time to think about all this. I am not sure it's a situation I need in my life right now."

"Anna, look I know this sounds bizarre, but MDH wants the three of us to meet up tomorrow to talk about things. Please, please come to London and do this for me. I need you now more than ever."

I didn't care how hurtful MDH found my words. He had forced my hand and I felt like a cornered animal. At that moment, my only chance seemed to be Anna and I needed to do everything in my power to convince her not to let me go.

"Wow, you and I haven't even slept together and you're already suggesting a threesome with your husband," she quipped.

The humour coupled with her change in tone came as a huge relief. She wasn't going to give up on me and for that I felt immensely grateful.

"Look, darling," she continued, "when we met last night I was immediately smitten. Ring me later and give me the details of this liaison. I'll arrange my work so that I can be down South tomorrow – I love you. Now go before I change my mind."

I snapped my mobile shut and looked at MDH defiantly. Getting Anna to agree to his odd request was a test he'd hoped she would fail.

"You're on," I told him. "Let me know where and when. Anna and I will meet you there."

"I want you to move into the attic bedroom, Alice. I don't want you near me again," was all MDH muttered before disappearing to The Shed.

I spent the next hour sorting out the attic, which was to be my sanctuary in the coming months. MDH sent me a text with the details for our get-together the next day. I got hold of Anna and updated her on the arrangements. She was so lovely to me on the phone, reassuring me with her Radio 4 continuity tones that all would be well.

Having organised my new bedroom, I sat swigging from a bottle of Baileys I'd taken upstairs with me. I couldn't believe how suddenly my life was changing and rather than feeling sad, I was thrilled. I must have passed out at some stage as I woke up at dawn still fully dressed and clutching the empty Baileys' bottle to my chest. My tongue was stuck to the roof of my mouth, my head throbbed and the stale air in my tiny new room stank of tobacco.

Dear God, I prayed that I'd not tried ringing Anna again after finishing the entire contents of the Baileys' bottle. What if I had said something totally inappropriate? On checking my phone log, the last call I'd made had been the one I remembered before getting poleaxed. Phew.

The day passed with a tedious torpor that seemed to sap my very lifeblood. Although nervous about how the evening would unfold, I felt like a teenager, desperate to see the object of my desire again. I needed a fix. Never before had my feelings for someone crescendoed quite so quickly.

MDH had come into the office that day full of false bonhomie, seizing every opportunity to ridicule me. Be it work, my staff, even the clothes I was wearing. Everyone seemed to retract into their necklines like a bunch of nervous tortoises.

Eventually the appointed time to meet Anna arrived. I managed to slip out of the office unnoticed whilst MDH was flirting at the photocopier with the office junior. He had wanted us to travel together to meet Anna. I sent him a text telling him I'd meet him there.

As I drove past the place MDH had chosen, I spotted Anna. She was already inside waiting for me. My heart did a little jig. It was surreal to see her in surroundings that were so familiar to me. I parked, checked my make-up for the umpteenth time and made my way to the bar, ordering a G&T before sitting down next to her.

She had chosen a table close to the window, but hidden from the view of everyone else in the place. She leant forward and gave me a gentle kiss that, once again, rocked my world. Anna then took my hand and stared intently at me.

"How are you, darling? I have been so concerned about you."

"Fine – all the better for seeing you." I tried to return the kiss.

She recoiled, which took me by surprise, but I didn't say anything. I didn't want to do anything to upset the woman.

We briefly discussed MDH's likely line of questioning but, if truth be told, I had no idea what mad machinations were going on in his twisted mind. Anna reassured me that, despite having lied through my teeth about my domestic arrangements, she wasn't going to let me go. My future happiness was sitting next to me sipping a glass of chilled Chardonnay.

MDH arrived and was professionally pleasant to both Anna and myself. He cut to the chase. He no longer wanted to be with me. His concern was for the children and he wanted to know what plans Anna and I had made for them in our new life together.

Blimey, I thought. As he himself had pointed out, we only met for the first time a couple of nights ago. How the Jezebels could we be expected to answer a question like that? However, Anna smooth-talked MDH, repeating the story she'd told me the night before about her previous girlfriend and how she'd loved having a surrogate family.

She also added a few new twists, and it was a somewhat different version to the one she'd given me but, as it seemed to placate MDH, I let it go.

As if planning a summer barbeque, we agreed on how to make the immediate future work. MDH and I would have the kids on alternate weekends, the house would be put on the market and divorce proceedings would begin with immediate effect. In the meantime, we would continue to run the business together until everything else had been sorted out.

I was slightly hurt by the business-like way MDH dealt with the situation without a hint of regret or emotion. Gosh, wasn't I worth fighting for just a little bit?

Having marked out the choice cuts of our lives as you would a pig for butchering, MDH switched into small-talk mode. He asked Anna about her work, her interest in motorbikes and the area of the country in which she lived. She answered everything without batting an eyelid. Eventually MDH became bored of this game and got ready to leave. I couldn't wait to see the back of him and have some more alone time with Anna.

Having watched MDH disappear into a sea of diners, Anna turned to me and smiled.

"Well, baby, you're mine now it seems. Let's make some plans. What are you doing for Christmas?"

Given it was the first week of June I thought she was joking. However, she went on to paint a *Country Living* double-page-spread of our first festive season together. It sounded enchanting and I imagined a future filled with sugar-sweet moments, which ran through my head like a theatrical movie trailer for *The Rest Of My Life*.

We left the restaurant and walked hand in hand towards the river, on the hunt for somewhere quieter to spend the next hour or so. Crammed into a cosy corner of a tiny pub, we talked about how wonderful things would now be. Anna stroked my face and our conversation was punctuated with brief kisses. I had never been one for public displays of affection, but I had no problem being so demonstrative with Anna, despite the shocked looks we got from some of the older clientele.

The sound of the landlord ringing the bell for last orders felt like a betrayal. Yet again I would have to say goodbye to Anna without any clear idea as to when I'd next see her. I slipped off a necklace I had been wearing – a chunky, silver heart on a chain – and handed it to her. She reciprocated by giving me her bracelet, which was more functional than romantic as it was magnetised to help relieve the pain of arthritis. Oh well, it's the thought that counts.

We walked back slowly to where we'd left our cars, fingers entwined and stopping regularly to kiss. I was amazed at my endless hunger for all this physical contact with another human being.

As I watched the rear lights of her car disappear over Kew Bridge, I felt my world closing down to a tiny aperture again. Anna, Anna, Anna. You have changed me, and my life, forever.

CHAPTER 5

Our lives continued in nuclear meltdown. I discovered MDH had given 'the troops' at work an in-depth briefing on my relationship status and my reassigned sexuality. This resulted in a definite sea change in the attitude of some of the younger girls in the office who now treated me with caution, casting sidelong glances as if I was some kind of predator. If I found myself alone with one of them in the 'ladies' or the kitchen, they'd nervously make their excuses and back out of the room. It was as if they were frightened that I would strap on a super-size dildo and make a pass at them. Amazing how prejudices are alive and kicking in a generation that should know better.

It was our senior designer who hurt me the most though. I had always been good friends with Naz and we'd often been for a drink after work to brainstorm ideas together. So it came as a shock to find him siding with MDH and giving me the cold shoulder. He joined in with the sarcasm then threw conspiratorial glances at MDH in a bid to curry favour. Obviously I was seen as the rank outsider to take over the business.

Although I had expected MDH to use my sexual proclivity in his campaign for office supremacy, his divisive approach to the children took me by surprise. He had disappeared from work early one evening without so much as a by-your-leave. When I arrived home, I found the kids lined up on the sofa putting me in mind of *The Sound of Music* yet again. They all had the look of rabbits caught in the headlights of an approaching juggernaut.

MDH was pacing up and down. As I walked through the door, he gave me his characteristically snide smile.

"Ah children, your mother has returned so we can now discuss the matter in hand."

"What's going on?" I asked.

It was crippling to see the pain on their little faces, all fearing they'd done something wrong and that big trouble lay in store for them. All because of MDH and his wretched power trips.

Power Trips

MDH seemed to take pleasure in exerting power over anyone or anything. Even when they were really tiny, if the children were naughty, MDH had thought nothing of publicly humiliating them. No matter where we were, he'd shout loudly, make them drop their pants and smack their naked little bottoms. I had been at my wits' end on one occasion over his treatment of my eldest son.

Aged seven, my little boy had refused to eat a second blackened sausage his father had cremated on the BBQ one Sunday lunchtime. MDH had made him sit outside for seven hours waiting for him to eat the offending item, even refusing to allow me to bring him a fleece as the evening temperature plummeted. Give my son his due, he defiantly shivered his way through to the point MDH gave in and sent him to bed.

Without answering me, MDH took centre stage.

"Your mother has become a lesbian," he announced, like some self-important ringmaster at the circus.

Flabbergasted, I couldn't believe this ludicrous situation. For a start, the kids had no idea what he meant by a lesbian and looked at me as though I was some interplanetary traveller from *Dr Who*.

"Your mother is abandoning us to live with another woman kids."

"Oh for God's sake, I am NOT abandoning anyone or moving anywhere. This is not the right way to handle this situation. Please leave them out of this mess."

"Your mess!" he shouted and lunged at me with a murderous look on his face, whereupon I found myself sprawled on the floor.

Terrified, the kids ran out of the room crying and bedlam broke loose in our House of Horrors.

Eventually I calmed the kids down, got them all in the bath and tried to lighten the mood by making them 'beards' out of bubble bath foam. However, there was no getting away from the scene they had just witnessed and they were all desperate to know what was going on.

I explained to them that Daddy and I loved all three of them dearly. We just didn't love each other any more. I reassured them once we had sorted things out, everyone would be a lot happier as there would be no more fighting.

Despite painting a future of domestic bliss, they all went to bed looking punch drunk and very subdued. Was I doing the right thing? Of course I was, I told myself. The atmosphere in our house was poisonous and had been getting worse with each passing day. I was too much of a coward to leave MDH without having a refuge and that's what Anna provided.

Oh God, I suddenly remembered Anna. I'd promised to ring her over an hour ago. I dashed up to my room and frantically tapped in her number – voicemail. I dialled her home phone but was greeted by that irritating posh BT woman telling me I was listening to a recorded message.

I was gripped by gnawing uncertainty. Why wasn't she answering? Was she out? Perhaps she decided to get together with one of the other respondents to her *Guardian* ad? Someone with a less complicated home life. Suddenly life had knocked every ounce of trust out of me and I taunted myself with suspicions. Jeez, I was my own worst enemy.

I checked with the nanny to make sure she was planning on staying in that evening and hotfooted it down to the off-license. Panic had set in and I needed a drink. Several of them in fact. I bought a couple of bottles of Baileys, telling the shop assistant, quite unnecessarily, that they were birthday presents. Oh the disgrace of excessive drinking. Where did it all begin?

WHERE DID IT ALL BEGIN?

Excessive drinking had always been one of my coping skills (my only coping skill, come to think about it) when dealing with my emotions.

I'd discovered my mother's bubbling demijohns brimming with homemade wine down in the cellar when I was a hormonal fifteen-year-old. I became adept at siphoning off large quantities and re-filling the giant bottles with water. My mother, who enjoyed a drink or two herself, often looked bemused at the lack of oomph her home brews proffered.

On my way home, I finished the first bottle of Baileys in a couple of gulps. I staggered up to my room to continue wallowing in misery. Between slurps and smoking, I managed to set fire to my duvet, which I found tremendously amusing in my inebriated state.

Having doused the flames, beaten the living daylights out of the squawking fire alarm, attempted to get hold of Anna a further twenty times at least, and exotically danced around the room to my iPod, I collapsed into bed in another drunken stupor.

I missed Anna's call when she rang later that evening. She left an apologetic message. She'd popped up to see her friend Arthur who needed some help with his new computer. There was no mobile signal where he lived, she added.

Waking the next morning, I found a note under my door from MDH. He wanted to spend the coming weekend with the children. He felt they needed his calming influence in the present circumstances. Oh right! That was likely to be about as tranquil as the last moments on the *Titanic*.

Whilst the possibility of spending an entire weekend with Anna seemed exciting, my heart yearned for my three babies. How would they manage without their mum around? The reality of my circumstances thudded inside my head and I felt a ripple of panic. Was this the pattern life was doomed to follow for the foreseeable future? I drained the gooey remains from a Baileys' bottle and lit a cigarette.

As it turned out, Anna was going to be away for the weekend as her mother was having a birthday party. I felt marginally disgruntled. Surely my disintegrating circumstances took priority over a family knees-up?

Instead, it was agreed we'd meet in her neck of the woods at lunchtime on Sunday and grab a few hours together.

I decided to go and stay with my parents instead – dad was my biggest supporter and he had no time for MDH.

Crazy Canary

My father had turned his hatred of MDH into an obsessive past-time. He called him the Crazy Canary after MDH's inane behaviour at my Dad's seventieth birthday lunch. The kids and I had driven down together for the celebratory do, but MDH had decided, as per usual, to use the opportunity to train on his bicycle.

He'd turned up just as everyone was finishing their main course, sweating profusely in his neon yellow Lycra and with his hair performing gravity-defying feats. Instead of apologising for his tardiness, he simply grinned in that special way which made you want to slap him around the chops with a wet fish.

I arranged to spend Friday and Saturday night with my parents. Although I was still irked that Anna hadn't dropped everything to be at my side, the thought of going home made me feel a bit better. I loved being in the countryside and it was always a blessing to get out of London.

On Friday afternoon I picked the kids up from school and took them out for tea, feeling like complete crap. Throughout the meal I reminded myself what a wicked harlot of a mother I had become. As I kissed them goodbye, I felt tears welling up.

"Don't cry, Mummy," my little girl said, hugging my legs. "You'll make me cry too."

Suddenly my whole body convulsed with sobs as I crouched on the floor holding all three of my precious little people close to me. I felt ripped in four. Desperate as I was to be with Anna, the thought of leaving MDH in sole charge of my children seemed cowardly and just plain wrong.

Our nanny came to my rescue, hustling the children out of the hallway to allow me to get on my way.

My mood lightened a little as I sped along the motorway in my nifty Audi TT. It was a gorgeous day, I had the roof down, the music was turned up loud and lustful thoughts filled my head.

Arriving late, I sat and had a quick cup of tea with my mum and dad before heading off to bed. My mobile was winking like some berserk robot and I discovered a host of texts.

There were several from Anna. They were long and passionate, filled with loving sentiments that made me feel very special. Up like a rocket, down like a stick. The next few were from MDH. Apparently, he had spent the evening with the kids sitting on the kitchen floor with everyone in tears. Oh God – bring on the horsehair shirt and the whip. What was wrong with the man?

My phone rang. It was Anna. She'd just got back from the pub and had felt a big love moment for me. She sounded a little tipsy and very upbeat. She suggested we meet on Sunday at an old coaching inn in the heart of Stamford at around one o'clock, giving me precise directions on how to get there.

After our chat, I fell into a near coma. I hadn't realised how knackered I was after the events of the past week. Having not woken up until eleven a.m., I spent most of Saturday lying in the sun and fantasising about Anna. Although I was desperate to sleep with her and experience sex with another woman for real, I'd decided tomorrow was too soon.

Sunday arrived together with the usual butterflies of expectation. I primped and preened my way through to my departure before hastily saying my goodbyes and heading for the East Midlands.

After leaving the monotony of the motorways, I arrived in Anna country and was overwhelmed by its beauty. It was new and unknown territory to me. Gentle rolling hills were peppered with little villages built from honey-coloured stone. Not at all the industrial landscape of D. H. Lawrence's backdrops I'd imagined it to be.

Arriving in Stamford was like driving onto a set from a period drama. I was very taken with its charming facades and its sense of history as well as all its intriguing little shops.

The coaching inn was easy to find. I scanned the car park but couldn't see Anna's car anywhere. After heading into the hotel, I necked down a quick G&T at the bar, ordered another and went to find somewhere to sit.

Twenty minutes later, I spotted Anna weaving her way through the crowds. It was the first time I'd seen her dressed quite so casually. She was wearing cut-offs, a tight T-shirt that emphasised her gorgeous figure and sandals. She looked stunning. My heart did a gymnastic display.

We said nothing. She sat down opposite me and took my hands, mesmerising me with that hypnotic stare of hers. Her skin was smooth with a hint of a tan and the perfume she was wearing intoxicated me further.

She asked whether I'd like to see where she lived. Having agreed that I would leave my car parked where it was, she drove us back to her village. As we made our way through little back lanes, I was amazed how turned on I was by everything this damn woman did. Even watching her change gear was sexy. Without thinking, I blurted out:

"I'm not going to have sex with you today, you know."

"Good, I want to take it nice and slow with you, baby."

Smiling, she reached over and gently brushed her hand across my nipples. They immediately responded by standing to attention. Oh God, stick to your guns girl, I told myself.

Anna's village was yet another picture-postcard treat. Rows of period properties with perfect gardens, a traditional corner shop complete with a pub and a church. Everything a good English village should comprise.

She turned into her drive and I was surprised to find us pulling up outside quite a boxy modern house. I could have sworn she'd said she lived in a big country property the first time we'd spoken?

Inside was also a little disappointing. The furnishings were bland. She had bought everything in a job lot at a John Lewis sale, she told me. She didn't seem to have anything that had travelled with her through life. It was very different to my eclectic mix of 'stuff' that I trailed everywhere including, a teddy bear I'd been given the day I was born.

She went to make tea and I snooped around for photos or anything to fill in the gaps about Anna's life and her past. There was nothing. Even the pictures on the walls were framed prints that would have looked at home in a hospital waiting room. There were plenty of mirrors, so any concerns that I was dating a vampire vanished.

I was so in lust with Anna, I folded my misgivings into a neat little pile and packed them into a secure box at the very back of my brain.

Having drunk our tea, she led me upstairs to show me her bedroom. My first impression was how masculine the decor seemed for a woman. Anna pulled me onto the bed and we lay in each other's arms, kissing in between my persistent questioning. I asked her about all her previous relationships, something I'd avoided up to this point.

I felt a strange jealousy as she reeled off a great long list. She had moved in with a bloke at the age of eighteen to escape from home. Her father had died when she was little and she'd had an on-going battle with her stepfather. Apparently, the final straw had been when she had driven home drunk, deliberately knocking down a lean-to he had built that day. She was ordered to leave home immediately.

After that, she'd been involved with a married man for five years. They'd repeatedly split up and got back together until he discovered she'd been 'partying' with women at which point he finally left her for good. Soon after that she'd met her first proper girlfriend. She'd lived with her for several years before meeting Janie, the only person I noticed she became animated about whenever discussing her.

That relationship had lasted for several years before Janie had gone off with someone else. Anna listed a further seven women she'd been involved with in the subsequent years. None of them had been important to her, but she admitted she couldn't stand to be on her own. She would rather be with someone even if they irritated the hell out of her than spend time alone.

Her last serious relationship had been the married women with kids. I learnt Anna had broken her heart by dating two other women in the last throes of their time together. She'd had another brief fling earlier in the year, but that had been nothing more than sex and a good giggle, she added.

Good grief, these gay girls seemed to hop in and out of bed with each other like nobody's business. I was beginning to feel like little more than the next notch on the bedpost. I think Anna sensed this and quickly reassured me that she'd spent her life looking for her perfect woman and that I was 'it'. I was the most beautiful creature she'd ever had the good fortune to know. She wanted to marry me. I pointed out that I would have to be divorced first.

But when you've been starved of compliments and affection for a decade, flattery, I am afraid, will get you everywhere. Any worries I had about Anna's colourful love life were smoothed away with her gentle caresses.

The next couple of hours flew by in a blissful tangle of our bodies and endless sweet nothings. Eventually I made a move to leave – I wanted to get back in time to give my children a bath and put them to bed. Anna begged me to stay for another hour.

"We probably won't see each other for a couple of weeks darling, stay a little longer," she pleaded.

"There's next weekend," I said, having assumed we'd get together at every opportunity.

"Baby, it's your weekend with your children."

"Oh," I felt my stomach knot up. "I thought we could all be together."

"Sweetie, it's too soon. They need to get used to the current circumstances without introducing me into the equation."

She was probably right. God knows what I'd do with them though. MDH had made it perfectly clear that he was not vacating the house on the weekends earmarked as mine with the children. And I certainly didn't want to spend any more time than absolutely necessary under the same roof as him.

Instead of standing my ground and heading back to London, I yielded to Anna's demands and stayed for more cuddles and another cup of tea.

I felt terrible as we drove back to pick up my car. I was anxious about getting home in time to see my children, but also sick at the prospect of leaving Anna behind. Two weeks apart when you're obsessed seem like a prison sentence. Neither of us spoke and when Anna pulled up alongside my car, my heart felt like it was being pulled out of my chest.

Tears streaming down my face, I handed her a card that I had bought for her. She lifted my face in her hands and kissed away my tears with a smile on her face.

"Ring to let me know you've arrived home safely. Now go, before I kidnap you!"

Driving home was stressful. The Sunday traffic on the A1 crawled along at a snail's pace and I watched the clock dismally as the kids' bedtime came and went. I knew I wasn't going to get home in time to honour my promise to them. I slapped the steering wheel with the palms of my hands in frustration.

Frustration turned to panic. I tried to ring MDH over and over again, but there was absolutely no reply. Although I'd spoken to my kids that morning, I began to feel concern for their safety. MDH's texts had been so gloomy yesterday. Was he capable of killing them as well as himself, like those terrible tragedies you read about in the papers?

Taking some risks, I drove as fast as I could. Inevitably, I got caught on one of those sodding yellow speed cameras, blowing my clean driving licence of twenty years. I pulled up outside the house after a journey that had taken two hours longer than it should. Typical. I should have left earlier and not allowed Anna to siren me into staying. What a bloody awful mum I was.

I was relieved to find no horrific murders had taken place, but that didn't help the fact I'd missed their bedtime. The kids were tucked up in bed and fast asleep. As I wandered into the living room, I could see MDH glued to the TV making spasmodic moves with the PlayStation controller.

He completely ignored me as I sneakily poured myself a large glass of wine from a bottle he'd just opened. I was adept at drinking out of view. I used the open fridge door as a screen taking a few slugs straight from the bottle for good measure. I then topped it up with some mineral water and added a few drops of red food colouring for good measure. I hadn't lost my touch since those days in my mum's wine cellar.

When I got to my room, I yearned to speak to Anna, but I was concerned that I might say something out of turn. I wanted to let her know that, in future, I had to leave on time. She needed to understand how important it was for my children to trust me if I gave them my word.

For some reason, I didn't think she'd be able to empathise with these sentiments. I sent her a lovely little text instead, explaining I was exhausted. I downed my glass of wine and gave in to sleep. Thankfully, I missed a text from Anna who was more than a little miffed that I hadn't done as she'd instructed and called her.

CHAPTER 6

It was my dad who came up with the solution for the forthcoming weekend. He booked us a 'luxury' apartment at Butlins so that we could have a couple of days enjoying the delights of the British seaside. Bless his heart, he did try.

I begged Anna to come with us. I wanted her to meet my children as soon as possible. Given the gushing way she'd always talked about the offspring of her previous lovers as well as her own nieces and nephews, I thought she'd be desperate to start building our new family life together.

She wasn't, though. She dug her high-heels in, insisting that I needed time on my own with the kids to help them through these early days. I couldn't decide whether she genuinely believed this or was making excuses. I carried a nauseous feeling around in the pit of my stomach all week. This only got worse on discovering Anna's plans to spend the weekend in the company of at least two women with whom she had previously slept, including heart-throb Janie.

My journey down to the coast on Friday was horrific. It was a hot sunny day and the people mover's air conditioning had gone tits up. The roads were really busy, I'd drunk far too much coffee and I desperately needed a wee. What's more, my happy-go-lucky children had morphed into the brats from hell – shouting and screaming, throwing things about and behaving in a totally unsettled manner.

Chocolate was smeared all over the car seats and the air was filled with the smell of leftover McDonalds.

In the middle of all this commotion, Anna rang.

'You're home early," I noted.

Anna didn't seem to pick up on my slightly bitter tone.

"Yes, I'm meeting the girls soon as we're off to some music festival. How are things with you, darling?"

"It's a complete nightmare. The kids are being a handful and the traffic's really bad."

I omitted to add that her planned soiree with the gay coven was the bloody icing on my sodding cake.

"Oh, baby, I wish I was there to lend a hand."

I came very close to pointing out in no uncertain terms that she could easily have been with me. Anyone else would have been on the receiving end of a real mouthful. But Anna had this strange control over me that had me behaving like Little Miss Submissive. I simply uttered some pleasantry in agreement.

I could tell she was in a hurry and, with the promise of a call around eleven p.m. to wish me goodnight, she vanished in a puff of pink smoke.

When we finally arrived at the resort, the term 'luxury' fell a long way short of my understanding of the word. Never before had I stayed in a place where you were expected to make up your own beds. The sheets had all the appeal of Poundstretcher paper towels.

On the plus side, the kids were now in a much better mood and their faces had lit up at the sight of all the gaudy fair rides and amusements.

Once I'd unpacked, we headed into the heart of the resort to find something to eat. The restaurant turned out to be a communal affair filled with rows of trestle tables like something out of *Hi-De-Hi*. There was a lingering smell of boiled cabbage and we were all instantly reminded of school dinners. We decided to give it a miss.

Instead we feasted on lard burgers, chips, candyfloss and lashings of Coke. A far cry from the dainty vegetable offerings proffered by parents in suburbia when my children went round for tea.

I chastised myself for being a terrible parent for the umpteenth time then lit a cigarette and scanned my surroundings for an off-license.

After endless goes on the penny falls, we headed back to our luxury apartment. No doubt the beds would have been turned down and a dainty little chocolate placed on each pillow. Yeah, right.

By the time the kids had finally settled down and gone to sleep after their sugar rush, it was gone eleven p.m. I took a swig from a bottle of vodka I had managed to procure. As I leant out of the third floor window of our non-smoking apartment for a cigarette, my gut instinct told me the promised call from Anna would not materialise.

I spent a restless night tossing and turning, waking on the hour to check my phone for messages. I managed to use every ounce of restraint to stop myself from calling her, but my mind was full of images that gnawed away at me. I wasn't worried that she had met some horrible and tragic end or was lying on her deathbed in a hospital somewhere. No, I was imagining she had met some horrible and tragic lesbian's end and was lying on their bed somewhere. I could do nothing to stop torturing myself.

I was a complete wreck the following morning and felt horribly grubby. I had drunk the entire bottle of vodka, but it had allowed me only a few hours release from my panic. I was dog-tired, had a pounding headache and was out of cigarettes.

Whilst the kids were still fast asleep, I made a dash for the nearest newsagent to stock up on cigarettes and Red Bull. What I really needed was a stiff drink.

When I got back to the apartment, my willpower ran out and I tried to call Anna. My hand was shaking as I tapped in her number only to be greeted by voicemail on all of her various phones. I tried the landline several times in the hope I'd wake her up – if she was even home, that was.

Despite my best intentions to stay in the here-and-now and focus on my lovely kids, I was totally distracted for the rest of the morning. All I could think about was Anna – who was she with and what was she doing? Or, who she was doing, more like? It was the most I could do to wave half-heartedly at the three of them as they appeared on their circular merry-go-round journey for the third time in a row. I tried to assuage my shame by heaping gifts and snacks on them.

At midday I could stave off my craving for a drink no longer. I bought a couple of clear alcopops and poured then into a water bottle so they looked completely innocent. I also managed to gulp down a double G&T at the nearest Bar Grot before taking the kids for another fat-filled meal.

During lunch my phone rang. It was Anna – or rather the shell of Anna. She sounded terrible. I was soon to discover she and alcohol were not a good mix and anything more than a couple of glasses of wine brought on a hangover of epic proportions. Many a morning I was left to amuse myself whilst she lay in bed, recovering from the effects of over-imbibing the night before.

Apparently she had only just come to and it was like talking to a halfwit. She had driven home completely blotto, decided against ringing me in case she woke up the kids, and then crashed out the moment she fell into bed. I was desperate to ask her if she had come home alone and whether she was on her own now. I wanted to lay into her – big time – for not ringing me as promised. Instead, my odious little other self took over.

"I was a little concerned, but when you didn't ring I assumed you were having a good time so that was fine."

Listen to myself! A little concerned, my arse? I didn't tell her that I'd nearly bitten my nails down to the stumps.

My dark cloud dissipated somewhat when she told me she planned to stay in by herself and watch TV that evening. We chatted for a while, but I was slightly pissed by then having drunk on an empty stomach. So I kept my slurred speech to a minimum.

Anna stayed in touch throughout the rest of the weekend with lots of texts and love messages. I half-wondered whether this was through guilt, but at least it meant I could finally relax and enjoy my time with the children. We sat on the beach that evening, giggling and sipping ice cream soda in between great mouthfuls of delicious fish and chips. Life felt good again.

My dad drove down to join us for lunch on Sunday. The kids loved their grandpa. He made them laugh with his silly jokes and off-the-cuff remarks. Despite enjoying being the centre of their attention, I could tell he was itching to take me to one side and impart some wise homily or another.

After a couple of hours, I suggested it would be a sensible idea to get on the road to avoid a repeat of Friday's appalling traffic (and to escape any imminent paternal lectures).

The journey back was a doddle. When we got home, I cooked my children a proper evening meal, got them bathed, read to them in bed and got all their things organised for school the next day. MDH was nowhere to be seen and I wallowed in the tranquillity of having the place to myself with only my kids for company.

Anna rang me as I was settling down to watch a video with only a bottle of sweet sherry for company.

After the emotional turmoil of the weekend, I was keen to make firm arrangements to see her. I was about to be disappointed again. Anna informed me that her village show was taking place next Saturday and Janie, together with the band she performed in, were playing at her local pub. Anna had promised to act as a roadie (groupie, more like, I sulked silently).

She would love me to come up for the weekend, but on the understanding she'd be a bit preoccupied. I was desperate to see her and wholeheartedly agreed to the plan even saying that it sounded fun. Was I being selfish? I couldn't work out whether I was expecting too much, wanting to spend our initial few weeks on our own together? I'd have preferred getting to know each other and trying to make some sense out of our future.

My spirits lifted when Anna suggested a romantic midweek get together. I was due to meet with a client in her neck of the woods and I could legitimately swing it to stay overnight. It also provided the perfect opportunity to spend the night with her for the first time. I'd already told Anna I wanted my deflowering to take place somewhere other than in her bed at home. I imagined the endless spectres of girlfriends past lurking at the foot of the bed scoring my performance.

Anna reassured me she had the perfect place in mind and would let me have all the details when I was on my way up. Roll on Wednesday.

CHAPTER 7

The big day arrived. My libido could have provided enough energy to power up the entire city of London. I was so sexually charged even driving over bumps in the road put me on the verge of an orgasm.

I don't know how I managed to get through my client meeting that afternoon. My heart was racing. I had drunk a large quanity of black coffee and felt completely wired. Nevertheless I managed to keep it all together and even got the sign off on a big piece of new business for dog food, much to my surprise (surprise at getting the business, not that I'd been pitching for dog food).

Having rung the office to tell them the good news, I took a leisurely drive to the hotel. Anna had chosen a place on the edge of Rutland Water – the largest man-made lake in the UK, she had informed me. It was remarkably beautiful. Mind you, given the mood I was in, had she picked a portakabin on a building site, it would have seemed like Nirvana to me.

I was early and arrived before Anna. I experienced uncharacteristic embarrassment when signing in at the reception. Anna had made the booking in her name – I wondered whether the staff suspected I was there for sex? I'd shared a hotel room so many times with my best friend Liz in the past and not given it a second thought, but suddenly I felt very conspicuous.

After a long soak in the bath and having shaved off invisible hairs, I did my make-up with the precision of an old master. I then tried my hand at a few erotic poses on the bed. There was still plenty of time before Anna was due to arrive so I ordered a sneaky couple of G&Ts to help me relax.

I soon heard a gentle tap on the door. It was Anna. She looked stunning. Her hair was immaculate and her skin glistened. As she gently pulled me into her arms, the smell of her perfume combined with the various potions and lotions she had used, had the effect of snorting something highly illegal.

I found it hard to remain standing as I experienced the literal meaning of knees knocking. Even her breath as she kissed me tasted sweeter than ever – fresh and salty like a gentle breeze on a beach.

"It feels like my first time too," she whispered in my ear. "I've spent so much time imagining what making love to you would be like, ever since I first saw you."

I expected her to slowly undress me there and then, but Anna had plans of her own.

Out of her bag, with all the flourish of Mary Poppins, she produced a chilled bottle of champagne and two glasses. These were followed by candles, which she placed either side of the bed before lighting them. Various other accoutrements appeared including strawberry-flavoured lubricant!

Having turned our hotel room into a sex parlour, she poured us each a glass of champagne, which we downed in one. Anna then pulled me towards her and kissed me passionately. I'd never enjoyed French kissing but with Anna it was different. There was none of that rapid fire in-and-out poking that I'd experienced with most men and which usually gave you some idea of what to expect from their lovemaking technique. Slowly exploring another woman's mouth with my tongue was astonishingly erotic.

Anna began to carefully undress me, deliberately taking her time. It was both torture and divine as she masterfully removed each item of my clothing. Her hands briefly stroked my bare skin and my whole body trembled. She kissed every inch, gently caressing me with her tongue, whispering how beautiful I looked and how turned on she was.

Anna knelt over me and stripped sexily. I was mesmerised as I watched her. She had the most perfect breasts. They were completely symmetrical, as if they had been created by a sculptor. Her nipples fascinated me. They were a deep shade of brown and reminded me of succulent raspberries.

Once again I was struck by the beauty of her lean, but feminine figure. She lay down next to me. Naked in each other's arms, we began to kiss tenderly again. The softness of her skin and the vulnerability of her body was another stark contrast to being with a man. I found her curves and gentle hollows so much more of a turn-on. It felt so alien and yet so right. It confirmed what I already knew. I should have trusted my sexual instincts a long time ago.

JUST A LITTLE CRUSH

My first big crush had been at the age of eleven when I fell head over heels for the chemistry teacher. Never had Bunsen burners and bubble rafts been so alluring and it was the only year I managed to score over 50% in a science exam.

I bumped into her, accidentally-on-purpose, at every opportunity even lurking in the school flower beds to watch her leave at the end of each day. I found out where she lived and made my long-suffering dad drive me past the end of her road on entirely false pretexts. I became a veritable stalkerette.

One of my friends' older sisters was my next 'pash', but she was a devoted heterosexual and completely oblivious to me as I fluttered my false eyelashes at her from the periphery of the disco dance floor.

There lay the error of my ways. I always went for straight women. Of course there was the mature skiing lady, but we'd never got past first base thanks to her husband and my mother. Unrequitedly lusting after someone from a distance is one of the most painful and frustrating emotions you can experience. Only overshadowed by the embarrassment of making a drunken, inappropriate same-sex pass, being rejected and then having to discretely apologise the next day. That's soul destroying especially if they are one of your own employees. Oh the mortification.

Despite appearing slight, Anna was surprisingly strong and more than capable of manoeuvring me into all sorts of positions around the bed. I was happy for her to take the lead. She turned foreplay into an art form and I hadn't realised it could be so pleasurable and last for so long. Her fingers and tongue discovered erogenous zones I didn't even know I had and she hadn't yet turned her attention to the more obvious ones.

She slowly made her way down my body with tiny kisses and flicks of her tongue. In the past, I used to plan the week's shopping or think about work when MDH was fumbling about the place. With Anna I was transfixed in a state of exquisite hedonism.

Shuddering in post-orgasmic pleasure, Anna took me in her arms, rocking me and reassuring me with a kiss each time my body pulsated in the aftermath of my climax.

My nerves returned. I was worried about having to make love to Anna. There was no way I could compete with her faultless performance. I began to stroke her gently and found myself once again entranced by her breasts.

I started to enjoy making love to Anna. It did not feel like a chore as it had done in the past. I inhaled the sweetness of her skin and wanted to explore every inch of her body. I tried to make eye contact with Anna to get a nod of approval. Oh God. She was staring into middle distance. I realised she was lying there like an emotionless first-aid dummy.

"What's wrong?" I asked. "Tell me what you like, what you want me to do, darling? I just want to make you happy."

She stared at me in an empty way before drawing me back up the bed to kiss me. She didn't answer any of my questions. Perhaps she wasn't comfortable talking so candidly about sex?

Instead, she suggested we should go and have something to eat as it was getting late. I was a bit taken aback. Eating food hadn't been top of my agenda.

Still glowing from my explosive orgasm, I decided not to say anything more about my tentative overtures. Besides, once we'd had a few drinks and a meal, she'd probably feel more relaxed and comfortable about the prospect of me making love to her.

Having not eaten in front of Anna before, I was worried about doing my usual party piece and dropping various foodstuffs down my front. Despite my very feminine appearance, I fell short in the ladylike manners department, as MDH felt obliged to constantly point out.

Anna ate very little. I was taken aback to discover she was "HKLP" – a phrase a friend had coined and the equivalent of calling someone a 'chav'. It stood for 'holds knife like pen'. A strange feeling reminiscent of the one I had experienced on first meeting Anna gripped me. I dismissed it instantly and told myself off for being such a snob.

We drank another bottle of champagne plus several glasses of Baileys and stared dreamily into each other's eyes, furtively touching hands across the table when no one was looking.

On the way back to the room, we kissed passionately and Anna showered me with compliments and sweet nothings. I was in paradise.

We only just made it back to our room before she ripped my clothes off, making love to me more voraciously this time. I responded just as intensely. By now, I was desperate to make love to Anna and experience the taste of her again.

Completely relaxed thanks to my alcohol intake, it felt intuitive and I was enjoying every delicious moment as I explored her glorious body. I looked up at Anna and realised that she had cut herself off from the experience yet again.

I could tell she was a million miles away. I didn't know what to do and went back to kissing her face and neck, which seemed to be the only thing she responded to. That night set the pattern for our lovemaking for the rest of our relationship. I was never able, or allowed, to make Anna climax and she only seemed happy when she was in control.

Anna did have the occasional self-induced orgasm. I sometimes wondered whether she preferred the anticipation of lovemaking but found it difficult to enjoy the mutual act itself. She was certainly very 'professional' when it came to performing sex, but how much pleasure she got from the experience, I'll never know to this day.

Anna fell asleep moments after I crawled back into her arms. Her tolerance to alcohol was certainly lower than mine. I lay there for a while in a state of confusion. I experienced such deep emotions for this woman, it was overwhelming and yet there was a detachment about her that I couldn't fathom. For the first time in my life, I had found someone I wanted to please sexually. Ironically, Anna was the only person I'd come across, as it were, who didn't want me to make love to them. I wondered whether it was a standard woman-on-woman thing and made a mental note to order some sex books from Amazon.

I had to leave at stupid o'clock the next morning to get back to London before nine a.m. Anna had set her alarm early enough to allow time for her to perform another round of mind-blowing sex. Waking up next to a woman is so much more pleasurable than finding yourself next to a man. There was not a hint of bad breath or BO and certainly no jovial farting. Neither was there the off-putting smell of acrid stale sex. In the past, I'd always done everything in my power to get out of any morning-after-the-night-before re-runs.

Afterwards, we cuddled and then drank coffee. I quickly dressed and packed up my stuff turning to look at Anna as I left. She had fallen back to sleep.

It was a beautiful day and as I drove back to London, I was filled with post-coital contentment tinged with a little sadness at leaving Anna behind. Making my way through the outskirts of London, I decided to call her. I was pretty certain she'd be up and about by now.

Her mobile rang out, but eventually clicked through to voicemail. I rang directory enquiries to find the number for the hotel, asking to be put through to the room when they answered. After ringing out for ages, the receptionist came back to state the blindingly obvious – there was no reply. I asked whether Anna had already checked out, but according to their records, she was still there.

My veneer of happiness faded. I couldn't understand why, after our very first night together, she wasn't desperate to talk to me? In my slightly hung over and forever-paranoid state, I assumed it must be something I'd done wrong. Was it because I had turned out to be a useless lover? Perhaps it was something to do with my snoring? Hadn't she made a joke about it just before I left?

When I got to the office, rather than getting stuck into work as planned, I spent the morning like Lady Macbeth, wringing my hands and wracking my brains. I must have left her at least three messages and tried calling her relentlessly.

As usual, my worrying turned out to be a false alarm – Anna called me mid afternoon. This time I decided to ask her why she'd ignored my attempts to get in touch. Didn't she realise how worried I'd been? She explained that she'd missed me so much that even hearing my voice would have been too painful. I believed every word she told me, and her explanation made my heart bleed for her fragility.

She quickly changed the subject to the coming weekend and Janie's bloody gig. Having made plans for Anna to collect me from the train in Peterborough, I made up my mind to stop worrying about her behaviour so much in the future. I focussed on my work and that evening, took the kids to the local park to play on the swings followed by ice creams all round. I avoided texting or calling Anna to give her the space she seemed to need.

Despite trying to behave like a grown-up, when I got home my smorgasbord of emotions got the better of me. It seemed Anna was still playing it cool. I was hurt to discover she'd neither rung nor sent me a text.

I knocked myself out with a potent cocktail created from the dregs of several bottles in the drinks' cabinet. I was rather pleased with the overall concoction. Having topped it up with the juice from an old jar of peaches in brandy lurking at the back of the fridge, it had quite a kick.

Never once did my behaviour strike me as odd. I assumed everyone did things like this in the privacy of their own home, didn't they?

CHAPTER 8

As Friday afternoon approached, I found myself in a now-familiar state of agitation. It was a creeping sickness at the thought of leaving the kids on their own with MDH as well as the inevitable guilt and dereliction. I knew Anna's hold over me meant that I'd be on the 6.05 Peterborough train from King's Cross. I wished I had more self-control.

Tears streamed down my face as I turned my back on the window where three apprehensive little faces watched me disappear down the road with a suitcase. I was abandoning them for the weekend yet again.

So why was I putting myself through such an arduous journey rather than jumping into my car? Only the day before, MDH and I had been through the embarrassment of witnessing my Audi TT, together with two of his motorbikes being repossessed by the bailiffs, as our financial situation got steadily worse. Thankfully we still had the people mover for family occasions, whatever shape our family was to take.

It was a baking hot day and I had to catch an overland train and then the Tube to King's Cross. There was standing room only for the entire journey to the main line station and my bleak mood was overlaid with one of sweaty irritation.

Thankfully I was able to find a seat for the final leg of my journey to Peterborough. As the train set off, I headed for the bar to stock up on some miniatures for the trip, even though it was under an hour.

I sent Anna a text to tell her I was on my way and received a gushing response. She'd just taken delivery of a vast bouquet of pink roses I'd sent her. I settled into my seat and knocked back several little bottles of vodka.

On arrival, as I disembarked I scanned the platform for Anna, but she was nowhere to be seen. I stomped outside and found her waiting in her car for me. Cheers love, don't worry about lending me a hand with my case or anything. Never one to travel light, I was worn out from lugging its vast bulk around for the last couple of hours.

I struggled across to where Anna was parked. The roof of her car was down and she was wearing sunglasses. She looked like a B-list celebrity and I felt my stomach lurch with desire. The strength of feelings I had for her still took me by surprise. Each time we met felt like a first date. I was crazy about her. I was desperate to get back to the house and head for the bedroom.

Anna seemed to read my mind. As I settled into the passenger seat, she leant across and gave me a long deep kiss much to the interest of my fellow commuters. The irritation I'd experienced earlier about her thoughtlessness towards me vanished.

When we got back, Anna opened a bottle of wine and we sat outside enjoying the balmy evening. After making short work of the first, she cracked open another. When that was gone, Anna produced some strange-tasting liqueur with gold flakes floating around in it. It felt almost as though she was deliberately placing obstacles in the way of any intimacy.

When it turned chilly, we moved inside. Anna put on a CD, lit some candles and I got ready for some love action. But she had other plans. She whipped off her top to expose her glorious boobs, turned the music up really loud and started singing and cavorting like some crazed cruise ship act. It was an unusual side to her I'd not seen before. Neither had I seen her as well and truly shit-faced as this.

Hoping this was some kind of weird foreplay prior to a repeat performance of the awesome sex of earlier in the week, I smiled and clapped. I felt like an appreciative mother watching a child making an appearance in its first school play.

I was becoming impatient. I had spent a good deal of time genning up on lesbian sex over the last two days, courtesy of the internet, and was keen to put the theory into practice. Anna had unleashed my inner gay woman and I was desperate to make up for decades of lost time.

All of a sudden, Anna came to an abrupt halt like a clockwork doll, which had suddenly wound down. She disappeared upstairs at a rate of knots. After waiting a reasonably discrete amount of time, I went in search of her.

She was fast asleep in bed and there was the distinct odour of sick emanating from the en suite. So much for my night of passion.

***

I woke the next morning to the smell of bacon frying. When I headed down to the kitchen, I found Anna rustling up breakfast. She looked somewhat dishevelled and her spiky hair was now reminiscent of a Bart Simpson do. Come to think of it, her skin tone was a similar shade to his due to the copious amounts of alcohol she'd put away last night. No mention was made about the unscheduled and sudden end to our evening. Sometimes the similarities between MDH and Anna were too close for comfort!

"Breakfast, darling?" she cooed as she piled a plate with bacon, eggs and sausages.

"What about you?" I asked.

She explained she suffered from acid reflux and could only eat small portions at a time. I watched as she poured herself a meagre helping of cornflakes into a small mug. I felt rather like Hansel and Gretel being fattened up for the kill. Since meeting Anna, my entire diet and exercise regime had gone to pot. I was certainly drinking more regularly as well as smoking at least twenty a day. This woman should carry a health warning.

I asked about the plan for the day, trying to muster an air of excitement and Anna wittered on about meeting up with everyone in the pub around midday. Oh joy. Normally I loved things like village fetes but the prospect of meeting Janie plus Anna's most recent ex-girlfriend was making me feel like crap. I'd have preferred supper with Vlad the Impaler, given a choice. I felt quite sick at the prospect and I was in no mood for a full English breakfast. When Anna briefly left the kitchen, I quickly scraped the entire contents of my plate into the bin.

After plenty of coffee and cigarettes, we both got ready to go out. I made a special effort with my make-up and spent ages trying to get my casual look just right.

As we walked up to the pub, I was aware how reluctant my feet seemed to be to co-operate. Around me, people were genially bustling between the various stalls dotted about the village. I would have happily disappeared into the crowd and let Anna go on ahead. But I was too jealous, insecure and nervous to even suggest it.

I felt like a fraud meeting all these "dyed-in-the-wool" dykes having only just emerged from the closet myself, albeit with great gusto.

Walking into the pub, a high-pitched scream greeted us and a small, insect-like woman ran towards Anna and threw herself at her.

Much to my dismay, Anna locked her arms around the creature and swung her in the air like you would a tiny child.

After their unnecessarily animated greeting, Anna introduced me to everyone. The limpet turned out to be Zoe, Anna's bedroom buddy until a couple of months ago. Irritatingly, she was still hanging on to Anna. She wore green sunglasses and I was put in mind of one of the extra-terrestrials from the bar scene in *Star Wars* – only a bit part, mind you.

A tall blonde girl gave me a hug. It was Janie, Anna's ex and also the lead guitarist in the band we'd come to see. Janie's latest partner, a girl called Suzie, greeted me with a huge, friendly smile and I took an instant liking to her.

Amongst the others gathered around the table were Jamie and Ned, a gay couple who had been together for over twenty years. Aha, fidelity at last. To date it had seemed a rare commodity amongst this particular gay enclave. The rest of the band stood around swigging pints and were far too involved in their playlist to bother with more than a cursory nod in my direction.

Anna handed me a bottle of lager, which I downed in one. I disappeared on the pretext of finding the loo and made a dash for the bar to grab another bottle or two of Dutch courage. After paying for them, I headed outside for a breath of fresh air. I stood and watched as three children walked past me accompanied by their mum. They'd had their faces painted and were happily bobbing along holding helium-filled balloons. I was wracked with contrition. What on earth was I doing here? I felt totally wretched.

As I went back inside, I noticed Zoe was sitting on Anna's lap, the pair of them laughing at a shared joke. My bad mood descended a level into abject misery. Before I had time to give them both the evil eye, I was pulled backwards and found myself sitting on Jamie's lap. His partner Ned made some wisecrack at Zoe's expense in an attempt to cheer me up. Bollocks! Was it that obvious how upset I was by the way Anna was carrying on?

I concentrated as best I could on talking to the guys and acting as though I felt completely comfortable with the whole fucking situation. Suddenly Jamie came out with something, which knocked the wind out of my sails:

"You seem like a lovely girl. Just be careful with Anna. She's got a bit of a reputation."

"What do you mean?" I asked, desperate for more information.

As Jamie was about to answer, the landlord announced the band was about to play and everyone jostled towards the back of the pub where a small stage had been set up. Jamie disappeared in a sea of bodies before I could interrogate him.

Instead of following the crowd, I visited the bar yet again and ordered further bottles of lager and a double vodka chaser. As I stood there in shock, I became aware of someone staring at me. It was a man in his late fifties with a ruddy face and dressed like he'd walked straight off the set of *Lady Chatterley's Lover*.

"You Anna's new girl?" he asked leaning towards me and nearly toppling off his bar stool in the process.

I nodded but didn't want to get involved in conversation with this man who was obviously drunk. However, he wasn't going to be deterred and slid towards me, putting his arm around me.

"Funny things, these dykes. Don't seem to stay put long. Anna's had more women than hot dinners. That little thing over there was her latest squeeze until you came along."

He wagged a finger in the direction of Zoe who was still bouncing around like Tigger on acid.

Bloody hell! I felt like I'd been punched in the stomach for a second time in as many minutes. Despite all the illuminated warning signs, I decided I would be the victorious one. I would be the one to conquer Anna once and for all. Hadn't she told me I was special, after all?

As there was no getting rid of him, I offered to buy my new companion a drink. He jumped at the prospect of a free pint. I was also hoping he might open up a little more about Anna. Before I could quiz him, I felt someone gently stroking my bottom. It was the woman in question.

"So this is where you've been hiding, is it? I've been looking everywhere for you. You've met Arthur, I see."

So this was the Arthur that Anna had talked so much about. My initial assessment hadn't been far off the mark. He was, indeed, the local gamekeeper. In the ten years she'd been living in the village, Anna and Arthur had become good friends. She cut his hair and ran a few errands for him and in return, he made sure her freezer was well stocked with pheasant and partridge. No questions asked. Not that Anna ever seemed short of a few game birds.

She shared his love of guns and often helped out as a beater on various local shoots. Personally, I had a real problem with any type of killing for pleasure and had been a member of the hunt saboteurs in my youth. I decided now was not the best time to mention this.

Bit of an odd friendship if he was prepared to badmouth Anna on his first encounter with her new beau (or was that belle?). Perhaps he had an ulterior motive? Was he secretly in love with Anna and his approach was just a dastardly ruse to scare off the competition? Alone and forlorn, she would eventually turn to both him and heterosexuality for comfort. Nice try, but my *Scooby Doo* storyline didn't account for Jamie being so quick off the mark to warn me about Anna too.

She dragged me by the hand to where the band were still giving it their all. Janie had switched to playing the drums (what a versatile young lady, I noted slightly bitterly) and another very butch-looking woman was getting carried away with a pair of maracas. She looked both ridiculous and bloody hilarious.

"Who on earth is that?" I whispered to Anna.

"That's Marta," she replied, swaying in time to the music.

"Have you slept with her?" I asked jokingly.

"Only once," came the unexpected reply.

I waited to see if an ironic grin crept over her face to suggest she was teasing. Nothing. She was being serious. Flaming Nora – talk about keeping yourself busy! Was there any gay woman within a fifty-mile radius she'd not left unturned? No wonder she'd had to seek out pastures new as far afield as London.

"She doesn't really seem your type," I said in a rather high-pitched voice as I tried to hide my astonishment.

"Oh, she's not; she was useful when I didn't have my car for a couple of weeks. She drove me around to gigs and things. She even wrote me a song – she was completely nuts about me."

Like an onion, layers kept peeling off Anna. Not only did it make me want to cry all too often, I found myself not really liking what was underneath.

Having always been a bit of a prude, I'd never been able to have sex with anyone without having first established a real emotional connection with them. Only once had I slept with someone who I'd just met and that was because I was completely trollied on scrumpy.

Time for another visit to the bar. Once again I found myself outside with a further stash of booze in my very accommodating handbag. I made my way to the local churchyard and slumped onto a bench. Oh God, I asked, what am I doing here? Help me please? I continued the rambling prayers of a drunk and ended up sobbing. I took out my mobile and rang home. My daughter answered the phone. Hearing her doing her best telephone voice only made matters worse.

"Mummy, are you crying? Don't cry or you'll make me cry too," came her inevitable mantra.

"I love you, sweetheart," I told her.

She asked me what I was up to and, out of the blue, whether I was with some lesbians. No doubt their father had been browbeating them with homophobic propaganda again. I waffled my way through an inconclusive answer and then had a brief chat with my two boys. Apparently MDH then walked into the room and when he realised they were talking to me, told them to put the phone down. With no one else to turn to, I went to find Anna.

Back at the pub the band had finished playing and preparations were underway for the evening's entertainment. Anna was chatting to Janie and Marta. I felt about as wanted as a thick sweater on a hot summer's evening. Not only did I feel miserable but I was bored too. The bar was closed so I had no choice but to go from table to table, finishing off the dregs left in any glasses I could find.

I'd covered quite a lot of ground by the time Anna found me and announced we were heading home with Janie and Suzie. They were going to stop by for a cup of tea. Oh, goody. When would this damned day end?

I chatted to Suzie on the way home and we had a good giggle about Marta and her maracas. At the house, Anna and Janie remained in deep discussion about a load of gay women neither Suzie or I knew from Eve. So we left them in the kitchen and made a beeline for the drinks cabinet in the sitting room.

As it turned out, I'd met my match in Suzie who was equally as partial to a good drink. We started dancing and singing at the tops of our voices. Having consumed a fair amount of vodka, our singing got louder until our mutual partners appeared at the door. Janie made a grab for Suzie, ruffled her hair and told her it was time to go home.

I turned to look at Anna. My foolish grin was soon wiped off my face when I saw her glaring at me. Cue the knotted stomach.

When the other two had left, she took me into the kitchen and began shouting at me at the top of her voice like a veritable harpy. How dare I behave like a drunk and make a complete fool of myself in front of her friends?

Fired up with booze I told her, in no uncertain terms, that getting drunk had been the only way to cope with her extended harem. I also added that it had been one of the crappiest days ever. She started mouthing off again, but I was angry, disappointed, disbelieving and not prepared to listen to any more of this rubbish.

I ran out of the house and down an unfamiliar country lane until I reached a gate to a field. Scaling it, I fought my way through the long grass and plonked myself down right in the middle. I felt alone and isolated. There was no one I could ring. I yearned for someone to turn to. Someone to give me a cuddle and tell me everything would be all right.

My phone flashed. It was a text from Anna demanding that I return to the house immediately. What else could I do? If I went home MDH would make my life just as miserable and I would probably regret being rash.

I knocked on the front door and Anna opened it, her arms outstretched.

"I am sorry, my darling. I know it was a tough day. I've had a few too many myself and I'm still very tired from our capers last night. I shouldn't have taken it out on you."

I also apologised for drinking too much and was only too happy to snuggle up with her on the sofa that evening to watch TV. We went to bed early and, this time, I was the one ready to crash out and Anna was the one with other plans.

She ripped off my clothes and kissed me more violently than she had ever done before. She flipped me onto my stomach, climbing on top of me. Rubbing herself against me, she dug her nails into my shoulders calling me names – "little bitch, whore, bad girl."

It was surreal. She was completely detached from her actions whilst I just lay there, still and silent. It reminded me of an expression we used to have at school if someone leant against you – 'Excuse me, I'm not your PLP [public leaning post]'. In this instance, I felt more like a PFP.

It was also one of the few times that Anna had a genuine orgasm, albeit self-induced. Having satiated herself she headed to the loo for a wee, got back into bed and without saying a word fell fast asleep. Wham, bam thank you ma'am.

CHAPTER 9

When we woke in the morning, Anna was sporting yet another personality. This one was tender and caring. Happily, I lay in her arms as she repeatedly kissed me and stroked my face.

The rest of the day passed fairly uneventfully. Anna didn't say anything about her angry outburst or her odd little sexual ritual the previous night. For the first time since we'd met, I was almost looking forward to getting away from her. That feeling changed the moment the train pulled out of Peterborough and I watched the slight figure of Anna sadly waving me goodbye. I yearned to be back in her arms and dismissed the strange events of the weekend as a glitch in life's rich pattern.

I'd managed to leave on time despite Anna having begged me to stay Sunday night too and catch the first train on Monday morning. More than anything I wanted to hug my kids and spend time in the company of innocents. Besides, the coming week was going to be a busy one, so an early night and even earlier start to the day was in order. I needed to focus on my life as a whole and stop allowing Anna to be a total distraction.

Monday started in its usual grim way with MDH in particularly good form when it came to irony and sarcasm. I bore the brunt of his attacks, but I was hardened to it by now and it had little effect. Anna had sent me a long, lovey-dovey email saying our weekend together had further strengthened her feelings for me. You could have fooled me. Whilst she wasn't exactly apologising for her roller-coaster behaviour, it felt like an attempt to make it up to me.

What completely took me by surprise was her suggestion I should bring the kids up to stay at her place the coming weekend. Apparently she was finding the two weeks apart too much to bear. What's more, she said she'd be happy to come down to London whenever it was my turn to have the children moving forward, if I thought it was a good idea.

Blimey, life seemed too good to be true all over again. I should have known better. Sitting at my desk at lunchtime, trying to get to grips with the pet food project and dropping salad from a ridiculously large roll into the unreachable crevices of my laptop, the phone rang. It was MDH. He wanted me to pop over to the pub across the road to meet with him and Naz. I assumed it was something to do with the same campaign we were all working on as they were developing the design elements.

As I walked into the pub, I could tell from their expressions that this meeting had bugger all to do with pet food. Uh oh. Something unpleasant was afoot. I decided to make for the back bar first. They'd assume I'd popped to the 'ladies' and I could surreptitiously down a couple of swift vodkas in preparation for whatever grim thing lay ahead.

Having knocked back one drink after another and with a third clutched to my chest, I joined them at the table. MDH picked up my drink and sniffed it in his typically disparaging manner.

"Drinking at lunchtime again?" he muttered with as much disdain as he could muster for someone who spoke in monotones most of the time.

I pointed out that this was rather hypocritical given the pair of them both had pints sitting in front of them. MDH moved swiftly on to the matter in hand which turned out to be... ME.

Apparently I was proving to be a disruption in the office and everyone felt it would be better if I didn't come into work any more. The famous 'everyone'. You could have knocked me down with a feather. How bloody arrogant considering I was the one who had set up the company in the first place and was responsible for getting most of the new business.

I said nothing. I needed to consider my response. MDH continued to waffle – something to do with paying me a monthly allowance until I found a job. Looking across at his fish face, I felt like planting a fist in the middle of his ugly mug. I also gave Naz one of my best Paddington Bear stares.

I asked Naz to leave. He didn't need to be part of this domestic holocaust. If we were going to lay our cards on the table, I wanted to show my hand to MDH alone.

"I've spoken to several estate agents about valuing the house. They can get it on the market in a few days. I've also instructed my solicitor to go ahead with divorce proceedings," I announced.

"Fine. Having got that unremarkable news off your chest, I suggest you go back to the office and clear your desk," was his response.

With that, MDH swilled down the remainder of his pint and banged the glass on the table with a dramatic flourish. He got up and followed hot on the heels of Naz, who had been lurking at the door, waiting like some nervous lover. Damn, that was a mental picture of the pair of them I could have done without. .

The first thing I did was to call Anna. I quickly explained to her the recent turn of events and she seemed remarkably upbeat about it. In a couple of sentences, she'd dismissed my concerns and suggested it was the perfect opportunity for me to find a job in the East Midlands. Why didn't I move in with her? Whilst I was still digesting yet another bombshell she did a complete about turn and started wittering on about shopping for the coming weekend.

"Anna, delighted though I am with your grocery arrangements, I am a little preoccupied with my career prospects right now to be able to have any input," I said in a jocular manner.

"Oh well, I won't do any shopping, then," she retorted before putting the phone down on me.

Oh for goodness sake, why was my life filled with drama queens and kings? I called her back and apologised, although I didn't really know what I was apologising for. But I had learnt that disagreeing with Anna was off limits and I was all for a peaceful life at the moment.

Over the next few days I focussed on my future. I actually found I was enjoying being at home by myself and the hours seemed to fly by, well oiled as they were by an accompanying alcoholic beverage here and there. A tot of whisky in my morning coffee. Or afternoon tea.

I rewrote my CV, which though I say it myself, looked pretty impressive by the time I had listed all my work achievements to date. That said, it made me realise that I was now a fully paid-up member of the middle-aged club. When did that happen?

I rang an assortment of recruitment consultants and arranged meetings with a number of them. I had absolutely no intention of moving in with Anna for the time being. Although the house was now on the market, it wasn't a good time for anyone selling and I planned to stay put until we found a buyer.

I wasn't going to leave my children and I certainly didn't want to uproot them from their schools to shift them to the East Midlands. School was about the only consistent thing they had in their lives.

Besides which, jobs commanding the level of salary I needed were only to be found in London.

The weekend approached. I hadn't told MDH the complete truth about my plans. I knew he'd scupper them. Instead, I told him we were off to North Wales to stay with my best friend of thirty years – the lovely Liz. Knowing that MDH was more than likely to call her to check on my whereabouts, I had inveigled her into my deceit and she'd agreed to go along with the story. Good old Liz.

Long car journeys these days were always a marathon of nerves. The kids transformed into gremlins as soon as they were strapped into a moving vehicle. With regular rations of sweets combined with the promise of a trip to Alton Towers the following day, I managed to establish peace and quiet intermittently.

Anna called me on her way back from the shops. Despite the background cacophony, she didn't ask how my trip was going and just moaned about how much food she'd had to buy to feed five people for a single weekend. I sounded as sympathetic as I could whilst trying to disengage the teeth of one son from the ear of the other.

Hours later, we were on the bucolic approach to Anna's village. On turning into her drive, she appeared at her door smiling and waving like Mother Christmas welcoming folks to Lapland.

"She looks like a man," was the first thing my daughter said.

"No she doesn't and don't you dare say anything like that in front of her. It's rude," I hissed through gritted teeth.

My little girl immediately scowled and went into one of her moods. Just what I needed.

We all piled out of the car. The boys briefly said 'hello' to Anna before running, uninvited, into the house. My daughter gave Anna a filthy look and stomped off, hot on the heels of her brothers. I gave Anna a big hug and made some throwaway remark about them being tired and fractious. She remained stiff and disappointed-looking. So much for her empathetic parenting skills.

Walking into the house, all I wanted to do was crash out and knock back a large G&T. However, Anna announced that she'd left out frozen pizzas and chips for me to cook for the kids. My vision of us all sitting around Anna's rustic dining table like The Waltons, warmly smiling at each other as she served up a delicious, home-cooked hotpot faded instantly.

I did as I was told but the kids weren't hungry and ate very little. Their priority was to make me feel as awkward as possible, poking around the place, meddling with Anna's electric guitars or demanding to play on her computer. It was incessant. I could tell it was driving Anna mad as she kept rolling her eyes to heaven. Rather than say anything, she kept pulling me aside and having a go at me, insisting that I 'do something'.

I was dead-beat and decided putting everyone to bed was the simplest solution. The plan was for the three of them to sleep in the sitting room. Two of them were to share the sofa bed whilst the other was expected to snuggle down in a nest of big cushions. Having got them settled, Anna and I went up to her bedroom to watch a film and share a bottle of wine. It wasn't long before there was a loud crash from the lounge.

I hotfooted it down the stairs in an instant. I was dismayed to discover they'd been trampolining on the sofa bed and my daughter had knocked over a lamp, which had smashed on the floor. I was in the middle of hastily gathering up the evidence when Anna appeared at the door. A knot the size of a football instantly took hold of my stomach. Surprisingly, she grinned and dismissed the event with a wave of her hand. It was impossible to second-guess the woman.

Eventually the boys went to sleep but my daughter ended up sleeping between Anna and me.

I was up early the next day as it was going to take several hours to drive to the theme park. I rushed around getting breakfast ready, washing and dressing my three children, as well as trying to make Anna's house look reasonably respectable. I'd hoped that Anna would have warmed to her role as potential stepmother overnight and given me a hand. Instead, she stayed in bed, drinking the tea that I had made and reading the paper I had fetched for her.

Minutes before we were due to depart, she joined us and presented each of the kids with a big bag of sweets. Excellent. Another en-route sugar rush to add to the already tense mix. I smiled lovingly at her and made the children enthuse with gratitude.

Anna seemed as excited as anyone about the prospect of going to Alton Towers. Personally, although I'd been a big fan as a kid, most of the rides made me feel sick nowadays.

When we got there, I increasingly felt like I was taking four children out for the day. Each and every one of them was tugging at me, wanting to do something completely different. It was like being emotionally hung, drawn and quartered. It wasn't long before I was wondering where I could buy a drink. I made a mental note that next time we went on an outing like this, I'd bring a flask of brandy laced with coffee.

The first ride was a tame affair for toddlers involving an excruciatingly long wait for a train that proceeded to go at a snail's pace around some rather unconvincing woodland scenery. However, my youngest son was thrilled and that made it all worthwhile for me.

As we made our way to the more adrenalin-pumping rides, said son suddenly decided to make a run for it. He scarpered in entirely the opposite direction for reasons known only to himself. Scurrying after my six-year-old, I cast one eye back and saw that Anna was completely oblivious to what the other two were getting up to. The woman seemed to have no concept of parenting whatsoever. I shouted at her, telling her to grab both of them and keep them there until I got back. I ignored the glare she gave me.

Not normally one for physical punishment, I gave my son a sharp slap on his bare legs when I caught up with him. His little face crumpled in shock. I was angry with everyone. With the kids for making this first weekend with Anna a nightmare. With Anna for not being the magical Fairy Godmother I had wished for. With myself for having created this whole mess in the first place. Reality overwhelmed me and I grabbed my youngest in my arms, rocking him until he stopped crying.

The highlight of the day was to be Alton Tower's big new attraction. When we got there, we discovered the two little ones weren't tall enough to go on it. I watched Anna head off with my eldest son and caught a brief glimpse of what I'd hoped our future would look like. As they queued, they chatted and laughed together, sharing sweets and really seeming to enjoy themselves.

I felt my heart leap and my annoyance turn to a feeling of intense love for this strange woman. It didn't last long.

Lunch was a major fiasco. Nobody could agree on where they wanted to eat including Anna. In the end we opted for the self-service restaurant, which was packed to the gunnels. I picked up the tab for the meal, just as I had done for the entry tickets despite the fact it had been Anna's idea to visit Alton Towers in the first place. I quickly dismissed any feelings of resentment, telling myself I was being mean-spirited.

During lunch the kids decided to go in for an Oscar-winning performance in the 'out-of-control brats' category. They refused to sit down and ran around the place shouting at the tops of their voices, no matter what threats I made. Salt and pepper pots were upended onto the table, giant bubbles blown through straws into their fizzy drinks and large globs of food splatted all over the floor.

People at the nearby tables were shaking their heads and giving me disapproving looks. Anna sat back and smiled in a conspiratorial fashion.

"Could you help me try and get control of this lot? Please, Anna?" I asked in as stern a voice as I dared muster.

"They're your kids," she shrugged and retreated to the loo.

Hot and bothered, I rounded up the kids and we went in search of Anna. After trudging around the park for another couple of hours, we decided to end our excursion at one of the many souvenir shops. I watched Anna hand the boys a pound coin each. My daughter had already disappeared into the stationery section, goggle-eyed at all the tempting pink and glittery goodies.

When she discovered Anna had given the boys some money to spend, she ran up to Anna and asked for her pound too. Anna stopped her in her tracks with an icy stare before turning her back on her.

My daughter started to cry and shouted, "You horrible man-woman, that's mean and not fair!"

Anna walked slowly back toward her. She knelt down and placed her hands on my little girl's shoulders and grimaced as she spat out her words:

"You should be in a borstal, the way you behave, you fat little girl. You don't deserve anything after today's display of bad manners."

I couldn't believe what I was hearing. I was so shocked it felt like time stood still before I finally came to my senses. I pointed out to Anna how wrong it was to leave one child out like that, especially since her behaviour had been no worse than either of her brothers. Anna was adamant she wasn't giving in and simply walked away from the conversation.

I knelt down by my daughter and wiped away her tears, opening my purse to find a pound. The additional promise of an ice cream on the way 'home' put a smile back on her face. I tried to make excuses for Anna by explaining she wasn't used to dealing with children. In my heart of hearts, I knew that Anna had chosen to be cruel and it was unforgivable. A little voice in my head whispered that I should run, run, run as fast as I could. If I had been a better person, I would have ended the relationship there and then. I wasn't though.

Once my daughter was happily engrossed trying out the various gel pens, I went to find Anna. I drew close to her, took her hand and gave it a gentle squeeze. With that one simple action, I had forgiven her despicable behaviour. I knew I was being a coward and I hated myself for it.

CHAPTER 10

Anna and I got a couple of hours alone that evening as the kids were completely exhausted after their big day out. They trotted off to bed like little angels.

On Sunday morning, Anna had another lie-in so we all headed off to the nearby playground. When we got back, I'd hoped Anna would have seen the error of her ways and had an attitude change towards my daughter. But the tension between the two of them remained knife-cuttingly palpable despite my little girl's attempt to placate the woman by offering her some of her sweets. God bless her!

I was pissed off that Anna joined in when the boys teased my daughter about her weight and called her names. But I did nothing to stop her. Spineless.

I did decide to leave earlier than planned though.

As I drove my now-silent offspring back to London, I felt miserable. The summer holidays were approaching, which meant the kids would be at home – something I normally relished. How was I going to make it all work after our dreadful first weekend together? My new 'idyllic' lifestyle was starting to feel almost as stressful as my discarded one.

A few months before meeting Anna, I'd arranged a riding holiday for myself to counter MDH's Tour De France fiasco. Following my week of equine solitude, the plan had been for MDH to drive the kids down to the West Coast of France for a family holiday at Club Med.

Since things had gone somewhat south since then, MDH had declared he'd take the kids to France with a friend. I wasn't really in a position to argue.

During one conversation, I mentioned all this to Anna.

"I'll come riding with you," she volunteered.

"Really?"

I was thrilled. I imagined all the romantic possibilities a week in France with Anna presented. A hard day in the saddle followed by a night of hot action in the bedroom. What more could a girl ask for? I pushed aside my concerns about the summer/ kids/ Anna equation for the time being.

Over the coming weeks I continued job hunting and daydreaming about my forthcoming French leave. The recruitment agencies told me quite a few companies were nervous about taking on someone who had been self-employed for so long.

But thanks to my witty banter and gay repartee, I was shortlisted for a couple of positions after just three initial interviews. One involved heading up the consumer PR division for an international agency's London office. The other was with a through-the-line marketing company called HellFire who were looking for someone to set up a PR arm.

I was rather taken with the latter as Tom, HellFire's ebullient MD, went to great lengths to reassure me it would be just like running my own business. He had a ruddy complexion and a beer belly, both suggesting he enjoyed a drink or two. My kind of chap, I thought. Their offices were just off Oxford Street and they seemed to have a relaxed approach to work. It all seemed ginger peachy.

The international PR company asked shortlisted candidates to go through a series of psychometric tests. Something I hadn't done since applying for my very first job. I remember one of the questions I'd been asked way back then had been whether I enjoyed hurting small animals? At the time, this had seemed completely bizarre. Why would anyone admit to that?

Ultimately, I can't have fared too well in the aforementioned test and I was not offered the role. However, Hellfire thought I was just the candidate for them and asked me to start in September. Perfect – I could use the summer to get my life back into some semblance of order and spend time with my children before knuckling down to my new job.

July arrived and with it, my first holiday with Anna. I had been fantasising endlessly about it, conjuring up images of romantic walk, hand in hand through moonlit fields of lavender. Picnics comprising crusty baguettes, pate and good wine, all perfectly packed in a hand-woven basket. And, of course, lots of passionate nights set against the backdrop of a magnificent French chateau.

I caught the train up to Anna's the night before we were due to fly out of East Midlands Airport. I had hoped to set the tone for our break with a romantic night cuddled up on her sofa watching a French film together. When I arrived, Anna hadn't even started packing so the entire evening was spent getting her stuff together. She must have spent a fortune on all the new gear she was taking.

Our flight to Nice left at five in the morning, so we collapsed into bed just after ten p.m. Despite having not started exactly the way I'd hoped, I was filled with anticipation about the week ahead when I got up at dawn. There is something rather magical about travelling so early in the morning when no one else is around. The sun seems to have a crisp edge to it and everything appears to be a little bit more in focus. Especially if you haven't had a drink the night before.

My excitement dissipated on arrival at the airport as my fear of flying took hold of me. The only way I could ever get through a flight was with a combination of tranquilisers and booze. Over the years I've had many an interesting experience whilst pissed on planes.

I'M DRUNK, FLY ME

I had spent six months working in the Caribbean with McBastard, a Scottish boyfriend with whom I'd had a mere dalliance in my early years. We flew out there like love's young dream and came back as love's inevitable nightmare. Our return flight had been overbooked, so McBastard took it upon himself to agree to being 'bumped' to a different flight. Instead of a non-stop flight to Heathrow, we had to island hop in an Airfix plane that was so small our knees had to fit up our nostrils.

At one point somebody asked the pilot what island we were passing over. He took out his map and, after squinting at it for a bit, told the passenger it was Barbados. Moments later, with a puzzled expression, he turned the map the other way round, apologised and stated it was actually Dominica. This was probably his party piece, but it put the fear of God in me.

When we landed, my nerves were shot to buggery. I spent the next twelve hours in the free bar downing rum punches whilst waiting to board our British Airways flight. We were upgraded to first class to make up for all the inconvenience and the free booze continued to flow. It would have been rude to refuse.

I reached that drunken state where you're absorbed by minutiae. I spent hours trying to figure out what the word le grest *meant. It was written on a button on the arm of my seat. I asked a very camp air steward to explain. With a withering look, he gave the button an exaggerated prod, my legs shot out in front of me and he minced off down the aisle with the parting words, 'leg rest, dear, leg rest'.*

I had come prepared for this flight and had a bottle of Coke heavily spiked with gin in my handbag. Once inside the airport, I made straight for the loo and swigged it down, accompanied by a couple of valium. As we were travelling ACME Air, we'd be lucky to get anything in the way of refreshments so whilst Anna perused the sunglasses in duty free, I sneaked a half-bottle of vodka into my hand luggage to ensure I had a ready supply. By the time we landed, I was pleasantly squiffy without being obviously intoxicated. I'd chewed a large packet of mints to cover the smell of the vodka – a drink, I had been misinformed that couldn't be smelt on your breath.

We were collected from Nice Airport by one of the staff from the place we were staying. Despite being reasonably fluent in French, I struggled to understand his thick Southern accent. I managed to establish we were amongst the first of the group to arrive and, on reaching our destination, we'd be shown to our room and could then use the pool or relax before lunch. After eating, we'd all be taken to meet our horses for the week, tack them up and go for a brief hack before returning for an early supper.

As we left the busy French Riviera behind and wound our way through pine forests and into more rural Provence, I felt delirious. The sun was reassuringly warm as it beat through the minivan window and Anna was surreptitiously holding my hand.

When we reached our destination, it wasn't quite the Disney chateau I'd hoped for but it was still very French. They'd given us two single beds, which Anna immediately pushed together and pulled me down next to her. We lay side by side in the quiet heat. The intensity of my feelings almost hurt as we gently kissed. Anna grinned at me and my heart felt as if it was going to burst with happiness. God, how I loved her.

We then showered, got dressed and made our way down to lunch. The dining room was in the basement of the old manoir and had originally been the wine cellar. The thick, stone walls meant it was gloriously cool. Our meal was a salad of tomatoes, fresh basil and mozzarella covered in an amazing dressing. It was served with great hunks of crusty French bread. Despite its simplicity, it was one of the most memorable gastronomic experiences I've ever had.

Another thing that had always endeared the French to me was their exuberance for wine at every opportunity. I was delighted to see a vast stoneware carafe on our table brimming with vino. Anna and I both had a large glass and I wondered whether being slightly pissed would affect our ability to ride? Could you be arrested for being drunk in charge of a horse, we giggled?

After lunch, we decided to go for a quick walk before joining up with the group. Anna held tightly onto my hand as we wandered through towering pine trees, which were oozing a heady scent of resin. The ground underfoot was a soft carpet of pine needles, crickets chirped in the background and the sun dappled through the trees. Utopia at last. This is exactly what Anna and I needed. Time alone away from the mayhem of our lives. As we kissed and she put her arms around my waist, I wanted the world to stop right there and then. It felt as good – no, better – than any of the fantasies I'd had.

Back at the stables we soon realised our holiday was not going to be of the relaxing variety. Our group leader and his sidekick, both of whom looked like members of a Gypsy Kings tribute band (all leathery, weather-beaten faces and earrings), were barking instructions at everyone.

In order for us to be 'at one' with our mounts, we were expected to look after them exclusively throughout the week, even down to mucking them out. No morning lie-ins for us then? To be honest, it sounded like seventh heaven to me having missed out on the whole pony club thing as a child.

My horse was called Pirate because of a black patch around one eye. I made some quip that I was glad it wasn't because of his wooden leg but it went completely par-dessus les tetes of the Gypsy Kings.

Our first task was to tack up the horses. Something I had never done in my life. Everyone else in our eight-strong group deftly manoeuvred the bridles over their horse's head and were soon saddling up. This included Anna. I was still trying to work out which way round the bit went into Pirate's mouth.

Anna noticed I was struggling and came across to lend me a hand, much to the irritation of Gypsy King 1 who was dismayed at my lack of horse craft.

However, once we were all mounted, I was treated to a toothy grin and words of approval for my 'seat'. I was surprised when I looked over at Anna to see how nervous she seemed. She was sitting on her horse like a sack of potatoes. Gypsy King 2 rode up to her and tapped her sharply on her bottom with his whip to get her to sit up straight.

Anna had often talked about the horse she'd owned when she was younger and how much she loved riding. So why did she look so uncomfortable?

We headed off into the forest and the gentle swaying of Pirate beneath me coupled with the goblets of red wine at lunch sent me into a trance.

It was a straightforward ride with just a single chance to canter. I heard Gypsy King 2 chastising Anna on several occasions during the outing because of one thing or another. Either it was her inability to control her horse, allowing it to stop regularly for mouthfuls of grass or for just lagging behind. I smiled warmly and reassuringly at her whenever I got the chance. It didn't seem to help much.

When we got back, she was in a foul mood and was mouthing obscenities under her breath as we untacked. Having put everything in ·the tack room, Anna started to make tracks back to the house. She was brought to a sharp halt by Gypsy King 1 and reprimanded yet again. Had she forgotten it was her responsibility to groom and feed her own horse?

She squared up to him and her eyes turned to ice:

"I'm a guest. I'm paying for this holiday and yet you're using us like cheap labour. This bonding business is complete crap."

Her words spewed out in anger.

Sometimes she reminded me of a rabid dog – one wrong move and she'd have your hand off. She turned on her heel and headed off, looking back to make a one-fingered gesture at Gypsy King 1. He shook his head in disbelief, spat an invisible something onto the floor and told us all to get on with our jobs.

I decided to stay with the group and take care of Pirate. I felt certain that Anna would be upset with me for not following in my normal faithful puppy mode.

Half an hour later the group – all French except for me – had finished up and we agreed to stop for a drink at the hotel bar. I noticed Anna lounging in the pool as I walked past so I went to see whether she'd calmed down.

"How are you doing?" I enquired nervously.

"Bloody rude Frog – I hate the French," she mumbled, splashing the water with her leg to punctuate her anger. "Go and change and join me," she snapped.

"I will when I've rung the kids."

"Always putting your bloody kids first. I'm sure they're fine and you're on holiday with me, anyway."

"I'll see you in a bit," I said, taken aback by her change in demeanour compared to our romantic walk earlier.

"Come in now," she demanded with the same edge in her voice she had used when confronting the Gypsy Kings earlier.

She scowled as I continued walking away without answering and mouthed "bitch" at me. Utopia had suddenly turned into Mordor – a barren land filled with fire and brimstone.

Instead of going straight to the room to make my call, I joined everyone at the bar and made short work of several more glasses of wine. My stomach was a tumble dryer of emotions. I also helped myself to a couple of cans of lager for later on.

As I dialled the kids, I peered through the bedroom window. I could see Anna still moping about in the pool with a sullen look on her face. Unable to get hold of my children, I went to find a quiet retreat to sip my lager and chain smoke before returning to the room to get ready for dinner.

I heard Anna come into the room whilst I was taking a shower. I was surprised when she stripped off and joined me. She touched me tenderly all over, rocking me in her arms and kissing my back. My head whirled with confusion as I tried to keep up with her changing moods.

Walking down to the dining room, I was once again loved up. Dressed head to toe in white linen and with a touch of a tan, she looked very sexy. I decided to give her yet another chance.

Dinner was served outside under the shade of a pergola heaving with a gloriously ancient vine covered in clusters of ripening grapes. We sat on benches either side of a trestle table and chatted amiably, helped along by the many carafes of wine we all greedily consumed.

I was talking to a woman called Sophie who was sitting on my left. I felt a harsh tug on my right sleeve and turned to find Anna glaring at me.

"Talk to me," she demanded.

Anna didn't speak French so I imagined she was feeling a little left out.

I asked how she was enjoying the food.

"It's horrid. Do you fancy that Sophie woman, then? You seem to be enjoying talking to her."

"Good God, other than vaguely noticing that she is of the female variety, I hadn't even thought of her in that context. It's just nice to be able to speak French again, that's all."

Anna pouted throughout the meal and, although she wasn't up for conversation herself, whenever I talked to Sophie I would get a sharp dig in the ribs.

By the end of the meal I was weary of her behaviour. Feeling sociable, I suggested, in French, that I change the music and we could all have a bit of a 'boogie'. It was still really warm outside and the huge veranda just cried out for partying. There was a round of applause. Everyone was up for it.

I headed inside and started shuffling through a pile of CDs. Sophie appeared at my shoulder and offered to help. Oh Lordy. Only moments later, Anna appeared and without trying to disguise her feelings, shouted me down and dragged me out of the room like a naughty schoolchild. As usual, I was taken aback by the strength her small frame possessed.

She frogmarched me back to our room and I could tell I was in for an attack. Moments after she'd slammed the door, there was a loud knock. It was Monsieur Le Patron advising me that I had a phone call. It was MDH. If Anna's looks could have killed, I'd be six feet under by now. There was nothing she could do to stop me accompanying Le Patron back to his office. Saved by the bell.

It was almost a relief to hear MDH on the other end of the phone. He'd spotted that I'd tried to call and had actually got the kids to call me back. Having chatted to them and blown them night-night kisses, I opted for the bar where the party was now well under way rather than going back to the room.

I'd only managed to down a couple more beers before I was overcome with a sense of déjà vu. Anna had tracked me down and I was yanked back to the room for a second time. And this time there was no timely knock on the door to save me.

Having consumed a vast amount of alcohol, I was ready to take on Anna. Instead of mild-mannered-me apologising for my behaviour, I went for the insults, full-throttle. My final remark, that she reminded me of a balding ventriloquist dummy, left her speechless. She pitched towards me and I knew she was about to smack me around the face.

I put my arms up in defence and she teetered, falling back onto the bed. She went into histrionics and made out that I had assaulted her.

Having lost the desire to argue and still compos mentis enough to realise we had an early start in the morning, I set the alarm, childishly pulled my bed away from hers and went to sleep with my back turned to her.

Bienvenue en France and so much for any passionate *Ooh La Las*.

CHAPTER 11

When I woke up, I experienced a few deliciously ignorant seconds before reality kicked in. The drama of the previous night replayed itself on a loop in my brain and my spirits sank.

I turned to look at Anna who was still asleep. Whenever I'd been through a similarly vile experience with anyone in the past, I would have been emitting waves of loathing by now. So why did I want to reach out to this slip of a woman and hold her in my arms? She reminded me of the pathetic remains of a baby bird my cat had once deposited at my feet.

I was unusually hangover-free although somewhat thick headed. A shower would soon sort that out.

When I walked back into the bedroom, Anna was awake and sitting up in bed clutching her forehead. She was obviously not feeling as perky as I was.

"I don't want to go riding today. In fact, I don't want to go riding again this week. You can go if you want to," she muttered without looking at me.

"Oh come on, it's a beautiful day and the ride yesterday was great," I pleaded.

I was on the verge of adding that the whole point of a riding holiday was to go riding. I'd been looking forward to this break for months and it was just the distraction I needed to clear my mind. But I knew anything I said would fall on deaf ears.

Instead I stood in silence in the middle of the room sporting my brand spanking new jodhpurs and a pristine Joules T-shirt. I did nothing but bite my lip. If I stood my ground and joined the group ride, I'd be accused of chasing Sophie. The week would continue to be acrimonious and world's apart from the bonding experience I'd anticipated. If I went along with Anna's demands, it meant I was weak, pathetic and needy.

I decided to be weak, pathetic and needy. It was the path of least resistance. Having agreed to abandon any thoughts of equine capers, Anna immediately cheered up, her migraine miraculously cured.

At breakfast I gave Le Patron a nonsense story about Anna and her back problems, which meant we wouldn't be riding that day. I felt like adding that I too had a back problem but mine was down to a lack of spine.

Over strong black coffee and buttery croissants, Anna mapped out our new holiday agenda. It involved hiring a car, exploring the French countryside and villages, maybe visiting a vineyard or two and perhaps doing some kayaking. I nodded in agreement like one of those wretched ornamental dogs in the back window of a car. Oh yes.

Monsieur Le Patron kindly drove us to the nearest town, which had an Avis car rental office. Anna chose a little grey Renault with air conditioning and suggested we each pay half towards the hire costs. I omitted to point out to her that I'd already forked out for both of our flights to France. I simply fumbled around in my bag to find my purse.

That day we drove further into the mountains and happened upon a picturesque village that seemed to cling to the rocky sides by its fingertips. Its main attraction was its church, but on suggesting we take a look at it, I discovered something else Anna didn't enjoy – sightseeing.

Instead, we ended up at a pavement café where I ordered a litre of lager, just to be churlish. We sat there in silence, both smoking one cigarette after another. What the hell was going on here? Was I doing something fundamentally wrong? Perhaps I was incapable of having a relationship? Do single children fare better as single adults, I wondered?

Eventually, I asked Anna about our future together and how we were going to make it work. It was something I'd not approached in such a direct manner thus far, probably because I was dreading the response. Especially after that first terrible weekend we'd experienced together.

She said nothing, raising one eyebrow like Roger Moore in a Bond film. My insides melted. How could such a micro expression make me desire this wretched woman, despite the fact I could have happily throttled her at the same time? I tried again.

"Well, how would you feel about moving to London? At least, until the kids have settled down a bit," I suggested in an already-defeated fashion.

"No way," she scoffed.

"Now don't sit on the fence," I replied, my sarcasm lost on Anna as she blew a haze of blue cigarette smoke into my face. "Why not?"

"Why not? Let me think... I love Lincolnshire, I have a nice house, it's convenient for work and I don't really want to live with your children."

So there we had it. Mrs and Mrs 'Happy Families' had packed up and left town leaving only the sound of a tolling bell and the occasional passing tumbleweed.

"Well then, I don't see how we're ever going to square this circle. Why on earth did you get involved with me in the first place if you don't like children?"

"Not all children, just yours."

Nice.

If this was going to work, we had to make some serious decisions. There were too many people's lives at stake just to let things drift, but Anna seemed incapable of dealing with real-life issues. She devolved herself of any responsibility for the current set of circumstances we found ourselves lurching around in.

She gestured to the waiter and ordered a beer. She was obviously feeling a little uncomfortable about being put on the spot. I asked for another litre in an attempt to further irritate her.

"Anna, we've got to plan ahead. When my house sells, I need to have somewhere for me and the children to live."

"You can come and live with me. Leave the kids with their father. Problem solved."

"There's no way I am going to do that."

"OK, so you buy a house in my village for you all to live in."

"Stop being so childish. I want us to be a family and live together."

She rolled her eyes skyward. Normally one for intense eye contact, she refused to look at me as we continued to bicker. After finishing our drinks, we headed back to the manoir as Anna had another of her migraines coming on. How convenient.

She went straight to bed and slept for the entire evening. Missing dinner myself, I stayed in our room with her and sat on my bed crying silently and thrashing about in my boggy marshland of self-pity.

A distant voice in the dusty recesses of my mind told me to cut and run, to pack my bags and make a bid for freedom. But I felt duty bound to try and make a go of things. If I gave up now, it would seem to make a mockery of the cataclysmic effect this relationship had had on a whole host of people. Someone had said to me in the first few days of meeting Anna, they hoped she was worth it. I needed to prove that she was.

The week continued in Groundhog Day fashion. The morning usually passed by without incident but inevitably I would get up to fighting speed at lunchtime after a few drinks, and attempt to talk about how the hell we were going to sort our lives out. It was like discussing something with a toddler. For a brief moment you think you're having something akin to an adult conversation. Then they'll say something entirely out of context and the illusion is shattered.

We didn't eat dinner with the group once that week, instead spending money we didn't have to at restaurants or buying food to bring back to our room. A gala dinner had been planned for the final night and I was determined to attend. Predictably, Anna wasn't interested and went into one of her moods, insisting on not attending. I think she expected me to back down and agree to do the same. This time I held firm and headed on down to meet up with everyone.

They were friendly enough, but having spent the week riding together, naturally a strong bond had developed between them all. I helped myself to a beer and went to stand outside on the veranda. I had spoken to the kids and MDH several times during the week and they, in turn, had rung me. They were on their way to France at that very moment. I felt gutted not to be joining them.

Reception on my mobile was a bit iffy so they usually rang the manoir. Every time Le Patron advised me of a call, Anna would grimace and make a fuss. I had been emotionally shredded all week. I knew that if my partner had been a bloke and was behaving like this, I'd have been off in a flash. Anna had a hold on me, which I couldn't fathom. The sexual attraction probably had a lot to do with it, as I was completely addicted. I was also shit scared of the prospect of being on my own. I felt a heavy sense of despair, which I attempted to drown by knocking back several drinks in quick succession.

I joined the others inside as canapés were being served along with slender flutes of champagne. Ignoring the nibbles, I took two glasses of champagne on the pretext one was for Anna. I drained both glasses on a brief visit to the loo. I needn't have worried. Endless bottles of bubbly were handed around all night and my glass never stayed empty for long.

The meal featured lots of large earthenware pots brimming with all sorts of home-made casseroles, roast chicken and duck dishes accompanied by wonderful salads and vegetables straight from the manoir's garden. Free from Anna's watchful eye, I relaxed and really started to enjoy myself.

As we were finishing coffee and liqueurs, the atmosphere changed almost as if the ice queen had swept into the room. Actually, she had. I turned and saw Anna standing on the periphery with her customary 'pissed off of Provence' stance. She had got herself all dolled up and looked annoyingly hot.

I prayed she'd relax and enjoy herself for once. She walked over to the bar and poured herself a glass of champagne, downed it in one, immediately followed by another.

I went over to the bar and sat on the stool next to her, helping myself to another glass too. She gave me one of those smiles that never reaches the eyes, the sort you gave someone at primary school whom you didn't like.

"Enjoying yourself?" she asked, not waiting for an answer. "How's Sophie?"

"Give it a break. Try to let one night go by without making a scene, for God's sake."

I filled my glass again and left Anna to brood on her own. I was weary of this constant feeling of angst. It wasn't long before I felt my arm being wrenched out of its socket as she wrestled me away from the crowd. I could tell from the glassiness of her eyes that she had got herself drunk very quickly.

She started shouting as she hustled me back to the bedroom. I was beginning to feel like Michael Scofield in Prison Break with my constant and unsuccessful escape attempts.

Anna locked the bedroom door behind us and stuffed the key down her bra. I sat on the bed with a growing sense of anger and stared at her. I wasn't going to be controlled like this. I traipsed into the bathroom, bolting the door behind me. I lay down on the floor, listening to Anna droning on through the locked door.

I desperately needed another drink. I wanted to get so pissed that I didn't give a toss about anything. I wanted to numb all this pain. Then a cunning plan dawned upon me. Tying an odd assortment of towels and dressing gown belts together, I flung open the second floor window. Attaching my makeshift rope to the radiator, I made my descent, James Bond-style. Well, not quite as gracefully. One of my knots came undone and I found myself deposited on the floor in a cut-and-bruised heap.

Too drunk to notice my injuries and the dishevelled state that I was in, I felt jolly pleased with myself and made straight for the party. I disappeared behind the bar to the store-room and purloined a bottle of wine.

Sneaking past the revellers, I chose a secluded spot in the grounds to annihilate my sorrows. The holiday had come to an end. It was the first time I could ever remember looking forward to the prospect of leaving France. I stared at the moon and the beauty of the surrounding landscape and wept.

I felt exhausted and although I could hear that the party was still in full swing, all I wanted to do was to go to bed and sleep forever. We had an early start in the morning and I hadn't even begun to think about packing.

As I climbed the stairs, I met Anna coming the other way. My heart began to race with fear.

"I climbed out of the window using a home-made rope," was all I offered up before teetering into our room and crashing out.

We had to pee using the wastepaper basket in the bedroom during the night as the bathroom door remained locked from inside. I felt myself being roughly shaken after what felt like only moments of sleep. Anna was standing over me.

"Come on, we need to sort out this mess of yours."

Having dressed and haphazardly thrown all my stuff into my suitcase, we scoured the grounds for a ladder. We found one down at the stables and carried it back, positioning it under our bathroom window. I held the ladder in position whilst Anna scaled it. It was a couple of feet short of the bathroom window. I watched as she adeptly levered herself up onto the window-sill and disappeared, legs akimbo, through the gaping hole. She'd done it.

I dragged the ladder back to where we'd found it.

Anna was in a completely different mood when I got back to the room. She greeted me with a big hug, stroked my hair and then kissed me gently. Whoooa! She caught me off-guard yet again.

I helped her pack and we went to find the minivan, which was waiting to take us back to the airport. Before leaving, we had to settle up all the extras with Le Patron. I was pissed off because I ended up paying for all of them. Apparently it was payback for my appalling behaviour, Anna had teased.

We sat in silence for the entire journey. It was in stark contrast to our arrival at the start of the holiday.

When we reached the airport, I found a couple of luggage trolleys, got out the tickets and handed Anna's over to her.

"Take this. I am not flying back with you. I just cannot deal with you any more. You don't seem to care what happens to me or my kids. I feel so miserable. What was supposed to be the best holiday of my life turned into a complete nightmare."

I watched Anna's face turn the colour of cheap copier paper and she started to cry.

I wanted to get away from her as quickly as possible whilst I still had the resolve to go through with my decision. A decision I hadn't even been aware I was planning to make. I was just as surprised as Anna. I started to walk away but Anna quickly followed before physically attaching herself to me.

"I am so, so sorry," she cried. "Don't break up with me. No one will ever love you like I do. I can change. I don't want to lose you. I promise I'll behave differently."

I tried removing her but she clung onto me like a frightened child. I then attempted to prise her fingers from my arm but she tightened her grip. People were staring at the bizarre sight of two middle-aged women behaving like pubescent chimps.

"Anna, stop this! Let go of me. For heaven's sake, just accept my decision and let's say goodbye with some shred of dignity, please".

She refused to listen, continuing to weep and wail. It was pointless trying to rationalise with her and physically she had the edge. I was trapped.

I gave in with all the breaking strength of a warm Mars Bar. Immediately Anna became attentive and effusive. As we sat in the departure lounge waiting for our flight, she showered me with gifts, duty free cigarettes and even a bottle of champagne to celebrate the fact we were still together.

She transformed into the Anna I had first fallen for and I basked in the renewed limelight.

Before my abortive break-up attempt, the plan had been for me to stay with Anna during the week MDH and the kids were away. I told Anna I'd changed my mind and wanted to go home for a few days. Without so much as a murmur, she fell in line and even begged to come too.

And so the rest of the summer holidays flew by. Anna maintained her new and improved self. I fell in love with her all over again as I was desperate to believe she'd turned over a new leaf. She even spent hours pouring over the Argos catalogue looking at kids' bedroom furniture and outlining her plans to transform her house into a family home.

Had Anna not made such a public display of her feelings at Nice Airport, I know I would have left her that day. As it was, despite her promises, after the holiday I never felt quite certain where I stood or which particular eggshells to walk on.

CHAPTER 12

With my start date at HellFire just around the corner, I decided to reinvent myself.

I'd been going to the same hairdresser for several years. My hair has always been ridiculously thick, falling in tight ringlets that had more than likely been dreadlocks in a previous life. Finding a hairdresser who could 'do a thing with it' had always been my personal Holy Grail, which I'd recently discovered in the shape of 6'5" Ike..

BAD HAIR DAYS

I don't know what possessed me to have a perm when I was fourteen. Thankfully it was the disco era as I came away looking not unlike a young Michael Jackson.

My next experiment came about whilst killing time when a friend was getting her hair done. Having always wanted to be blonde, I decided to dip my toe in the water with a single streak at the front. I ended up with a two-inch peroxide landing strip right through my middle parting, which earned me the name Skunk for the rest of my time at university.

Ike always managed to make my hair look great. I explained I was starting a new job and wanted something to give me 'presence'. He suggested prostitute-red highlights for a start. Well that should do it. For added sophistication, he blow-dried my hair straight. I hardly recognised myself in the mirror, all Sixties-chick looking. I was chuffed to pieces. I got Ike to take a picture of me on my mobile and sent it off to Anna.

Hours later she rang me to ask how much I'd paid for "that aberration?" When I told her, she indignantly suggested I'd wasted my money. Next time she'd book me in with her hairdresser in Stamford. Thanks for the vote of confidence darling. But I knew better than to retaliate with a cheap jibe.

Anyway, I began working at HellFire and for the rest of the year I was flavour of the month. I knuckled down, brought in lots of new business and carefully avoided any social events where alcohol might prove a problem. I got my life back into some kind of routine and even managed a trip to the gym every day and lost all the weight I'd piled on over the last few months.

Despite being the occasional arse, Anna maintained a well-behaved façade. She stuck to her promise of coming down to London every other weekend and made an effort to be nice to the kids. She was rarely moody and had gone back to sending me love emails and texts. I felt happy.

The housing market had plummeted so there was no sign of a buyer for our house coming along in the near future. Secretly I felt relieved as this meant I didn't have to make any major decisions and our lives could coast along in a relatively uncomplicated fashion.

As Christmas approached, MDH and I agreed that the kids should spend the big day with me. MDH wanted to go away skiing and even suggested Anna should stay at the house, which I knew was his insurance policy to ensure his plans wouldn't be derailed. Anna had never once mentioned the idea of us all going to hers since the White Christmas scenario she'd painted on our second date.

The weekend before the big day, she had invited me to go with her to visit her mother in Norfolk. A long winter weekend at the seaside sounded the perfect antidote to all the festive madness.

I left work early to catch a train to Norwich where Anna had arranged to pick me up from the station. On the drive to her mum's, we stopped at a little wooden hut masquerading as a roadside café, hidden from the main road by a thicket of pine trees. It sold every possible combination of sausage, bacon and eggs along with huge slices of homemade cake, giant pasties and all sorts of artery-hardening fare.

Even though it was December, the sun was out and we sat outside, whilst I ate a bacon buttie accompanied by a massive mug of sweet coffee and Anna picked at my crumbs like a disgruntled pigeon..

She seemed childishly keen to show me the area where she had grown up. I'd never been to Norfolk before and was rather taken with the neat villages and their rows of shingled cottages.

We found a stretch of beach, took our shoes off and ran down to the sea. Anna drew a giant heart in the sand with a stick and scrawled our initials inside it before taking me in her arms to kiss me. The taste of the sea on her lips made the moment even more memorable and I pictured myself in the grip of a gay mermaid. Bugger my imagination, it so often ruins an otherwise perfect scenario.

We walked past rows of candy-coloured beach huts, collecting shells and pebbles, which we crammed into our pockets. A small café near the front was open for business so we ordered two huge 99s. It was these idyllic moments that I lived for, that allowed me to bob along in Anna's turbulent wake waiting to be intermittently rescued. She did romance so well. Better than any man I'd ever known.

I hadn't met Anna's mother, Mavis, before, so I was a little nervous. In fact I hadn't met any of her relatives. She didn't seem that close to anyone in her family. She had several siblings, but she hardly ever saw them and didn't seem to speak to them on the phone either. She always bemoaned the fact her mother would visit her brothers and sisters, yet never came to stay with her. Apparently, she had very much been a 'Daddy's girl'.

Mavis was standing at the door of her bungalow to welcome us. She was a little Norfolk dumpling of an old lady with a soft, buttery accent and bright, dark eyes like a field mouse.

We sat in the kitchen and drank tea accompanied by vast cheese scones. The day was proving to be a real diet buster. The pair caught up on family gossip so I took in my surroundings. Everywhere was pristine and there were lots of trinkets, holiday souvenirs and things obviously treasured for their memories. I was struck by the difference between Anna's house and her mother's home.

After being shown our room, we all headed down to the pub for a game of darts before heading back for yet another intake of calories – massive helpings of traditional steak and kidney pudding. I deliberately drank very little, even though Mavis had invited us to help ourselves from the bar, which her second husband had built into the corner of the tiny living room. I could just imagine my mother's contempt at the kitchness of such an installation, complete with hand pumps and optics.

Anna and I went to bed early, as she'd planned another full itinerary for us both the next day. This included a trip to one of the largest discount shops I'd ever experienced, which proved to be an Aladdin's cave. Always one for a bargain, I was a reverse snob when it came to clothes. No designer labels for me. I was far happier to boast '£4.99 from the charity shop, don't you know?'

In the afternoon, we played a game of crazy golf and messed about at the local amusements. Another blissfully carefree day lifted straight from a gay Mills & Boone book.

That night, Anna had arranged for us to take Mavis out to dinner at a local restaurant renowned for its gigantic portions...wasn't everywhere in Norfolk?

Just as we arrived at the place, my mobile rang. It was MDH. He was off on his skiing holiday the next day and had organised a friend to stay with the kids overnight. Apparently, she'd had to cancel for some reason or another, on top of which my youngest son had come down with a fever and was asking for his mum. Could I come home, MDH wanted to know? Absolutely. Without hesitation, I promised to be on the first train to London the very next morning.

As I was winding up the call, Anna barged out of the pub door. Gone were the sweet and tender looks and instead she was grimacing at me. Although I was still talking, she started mouthing off at me, reprimanding me for being so rude. My stomach began to knit itself into knots as she disappeared back inside.

I finished my call and joined the pair of them at the table. Anna was already on her second large sherry.

"Who was that?" she demanded.

I sat down.

"I'm ever so sorry, but I'm going to have to cut my visit short. For a start, my youngest isn't well and also MDH's babysitter for tomorrow night has let him down. He's off skiing," I explained to Mavis.

"Well, he'll just have to go on holiday a day later – it's simple," Anna huffed.

"It's not that straightforward when you're booked on a package holiday. Besides, I want to make sure my little boy is OK. He's been asking for me. Kids need their mum when they're not well."

I addressed my comments to Mavis, hoping for a bit of support.

She nodded silently before getting up and scurrying off to the bar like a retreating sheep. Although I could have happily knocked back an entire drinks' cabinet at that moment, I stuck to my promise not to drink. Anna was giving me a Vulcan death stare when I caught her eye and muttering obscenities at me. She leaned across the table until her face was inches from mine and through clenched teeth, unleashed a whiplash attack.

"This is my weekend, you're with me and you're going to stay here until Monday as planned, you bitch. How dare you spoil my mum's night out, you selfish cow. Time to choose: MDH or me."

"For fuck's sake, shut up!" I responded in a hushed tone. "It's not about MDH or making a choice, it's about doing the right thing."

She managed to get another "bitch" and a few other expletives in before Mavis tottered back, still looking terrified. She'd obviously been caught in the crossfire of one of Anna's outbursts before.

As soon as I could, I headed to the loo to make a call to find out about train times. I was going to have to get to Norwich for nine in the morning to catch the only direct train to London. It was going to take hours. Not only was it a Sunday but there were also engineering works to contend with. Would Anna get over herself and drive me to the station, I wondered?

Back at the table, Mavis tucked into her food in silence whilst Anna quaffed glass after glass of wine, occasionally nibbling at something on her plate. Anna was a feeder, which stemmed from her early years as an anorexic. She liked to watch others consume large quantities of horribly unhealthy food whilst she ate very little. It was nothing to do with acid reflux, as it turned out.

Being with Anna was like having a weekly subscription to Ripley's Believe It Or Not magazine – there was always something strange and interesting to discover.

She had been a self-harmer as a child. I'd not met one of those before, I have to say. Her arms were criss-crossed with hundreds of tiny scars where she'd deliberately cut herself. I was fascinated but, whenever I tried to talk about it, she got very defensive, covered up her arms and changed the subject.

Then there was the time a family of mice managed to enrage her. They'd had the audacity to make themselves at home in a bale of hay in her shed. The hay was for her precious rabbit (more on this later) and she was livid. I couldn't believe my eyes when she took up guard duty just outside the shed on an upturned bucket. With the door wide open, she positioned her air rifle and took pot shots at the mice whenever she glimpsed movement. Try as I might, I couldn't get her to see the insanity of the situation.

I also learnt about a peculiar party game she'd played with a couple from the village after dinner at Arthur's one night. It involved the men present guessing how many CDs each of the women could stack on one of their nipples. The girls then obliged with Anna being the ultimate winner. Makes a change from Trivial Pursuit, I suppose.

Sod it. Anna was not going to threaten me into submission on this.

"Mavis, is there a taxi firm you know in your village? I'll need to leave early to catch a train at nine from Norwich." I said artificially, annunciating each word very deliberately as a cue for Anna.

We both looked at her, waiting for the offer of a lift to be made, but she remained stony-faced and silent.

"Of course my dear. I'll find the number for you when we get back," Mavis replied kindly.

I stared at Anna to see whether she'd change her mind, but I knew hell would freeze over before she did anything that smacked of helping MDH.

"Thanks Mavis," I added, giving her my sweetest smile.

The meal came to an end not a moment too soon. As I was the only one who'd not had a drink, I volunteered to drive back. Anna monopolised her mother on the way home as if they were the only two in the car. It was a relief, but fuck you Anna.

As soon as we got into the house, I reminded Mavis about the phone number for the taxi and made swift work of my booking. I needed to be up at six a.m. to be ready in time. Thank goodness I was stone cold sober.

Meanwhile I could hear Anna furiously at work in the bar, pouring herself one drink after another. I made myself a cup of tea, said goodnight to Mavis and tried to disappear off to bed. I was hoping Anna would drink herself into oblivion before making it to bed.

No such luck. She managed to stagger into the bedroom, deliver more of her rancour and give me a good shake before she passed out, fully dressed. As she lay there snoring, I was tempted to draw a goatee on her chin, fashion some horns from a handy floral decoration and take some candid shots on my mobile. She seemed the very essence of Beelzebub that night. What was I doing with this woman?

Once Mavis had gone to bed, I tiptoed to the bar, found a near-empty bottle of brandy and filled it with a shot of just about everything on offer. I was going to have to bolster myself with booze to get through the coming forty-eight hours. I knew the moment that I left Anna , my mind would start playing its usual tricks and I'd end up feeling guilty about my decision to go home.

Why didn't I have the strength to say enough is enough and let her go? The thought of Anna not being in my life made me feel sick and, instead of doing something revengeful, I leant over to kiss her forehead before falling into a restless sleep.

CHAPTER 13

As I'd anticipated, Anna remained furious about my decision to 'leave her in the lurch' and I didn't hear from her for days following my curtailed trip to Norfolk. Rather than letting her 'baste in her own gravy', I persisted in calling her and leaving increasingly pathetic messages, apologising for being so inconsiderate. I felt like I was turning into that unctuous Dickens' character Uriah Heep, which made me loathe myself further.

There were only a few days to go before Christmas and I had no idea whether Anna was going to grace us with her presence or not. Keeping me in limbo seemed to be one of her favoured methods of control. Being a great one for planning and making lists, I'd always find any arrangements hindered by Anna who'd often refuse to commit to a specific time or even day. It depended on whether I had behaved myself, she would say.

Although distracted, I threw what was available of myself into making nativity costumes, buying last-minute stocking fillers and putting up decorations. Normally I loved Christmas but this year it had the all the appeal of congealed turkey fat.

Anna finally got in touch to let me know she was on her way, just hours before my youngest was due to debut in his school Christmas play. She made a big thing about the mountain of presents she'd got for the kids. I was over the moon and cooed appreciatively. I would have

Anna by my side after all as I watched my son in his non-starring role as one of Santa's helpers.

Although we were late, the play hadn't started by the time we got to the school. That said, there was standing room only, so we squeezed in at the back. Being so close to each other yet unable to touch heightened the electricity that pulsated between us. It was another of the most memorable and addictive natural highs I had ever felt.

My high was quickly lowered when a row of small dwarves marched into the gym singing *Heigh Ho* in various keys of off. I spotted my son at the very back, one pointy ear slightly askew and the bobble on his hat bouncing directly over his nose.

The bouncing bobble remained his focus throughout the play – a trend that caught on with the entire dwarf brigade, much to the irritation of a large, red-faced teacher bashing out tunes on the piano. A row of little heads nodded in time to the music as reliably as any metronome (there's a terrible pun in there somewhere).

I was glad the play was reasonably short otherwise I would have had a real problem controlling myself. The bobble episode, combined with my sexual frustration, had made me feel like a naughty school girl on the brink of giggles in assembly.

On the way home, Anna and I swung my son between us. Maybe, just maybe, she'd realised she'd been in the wrong and things would change from now on. Perhaps we had a real chance of being a proper family and giving my kids a shot at the stability they deserved.

The following day was Christmas Eve, which was filled with a flurry of shopping and preparations for the big day itself.

In the evening, having put the kids to bed, I needed to finish wrapping all their stocking presents. I settled Anna down in front of the TV to watch her favourite soaps. Never before had I met anyone that avidly devoured these nightly offerings, refusing to miss a single episode. I had been more of an *Archers'* fan once upon a time, but I didn't seem to have the patience to listen to a whole episode these days.

I still had a massive pile of presents to wrap by the time Anna came to find me once her nightly viewing had ended. She offered to help, but couldn't resist having a dig at how OTT I had gone with the gifts. It was true – no doubt trying to assuage my guilt with an excess of shop-bought joy.

We polished off three bottles of champagne and a small sliver of Christmas goodwill must have been at work as we'd managed an entire day without any major ding-dongs concerning the kids.

***

It's when a small child clambers over your weary bones at five in the morning you become all too aware you have the hangover from hell.

Peering out of one bleary eye, I could just make out three little figures standing at the end of the bed, each excitedly clasping a bulging red laundry sack. Another Christmas Day was upon us.

We all tiptoed warily out of the room, leaving the sleeping Anna in a virtual coma. I had instructed my children on how to maintain equilibrium in her presence.

Downstairs in the kitchen, a riot of cheap paper commenced. I decided a hair of the dog was called for and opted for a Buck's Fizz – short on the buck and long on the fizz.

Normally our family tradition meant everyone took turns to open a present accompanied by a chorus of 'oohs' and 'aahs' from the onlookers. This had gone by the board this year. The children looked like little cavemen voraciously feeding on an animal. As one present was unwrapped, it was tossed aside without so much as a glance, never mind an 'ooh'.

As they reached the end of their seemingly bottomless sacks, all three begged to move on to the presents piled under the Christmas tree. I resolutely refused. I insisted on our festive breakfast of Variety Cereals, smoked salmon, scrambled eggs and a selection of M&S goodies before this could take place.

"Oh, go on, sweetie. Let them open their presents if they want to."

I turned to see Anna leaning in the doorway, looking slightly ashen.

"No, they've got all these things to play with at the moment," I argued.

"It's Christmas – let them. Go on, kids."

She ushered them towards the tree and they needed no further encouragement.

I glared at Anna who simply smiled back at me. She took my hand and pulled me out into the hall.

"It means we can open our presents all alone, darling. Much more romantic."

"Oh no, I am not leaving that lot unattended. Besides, I want to see their faces when they are opening everything."

"You've been with them all morning. It's my time now," she purred.

And, as my feet of clay caved in beneath me, I went upstairs with Anna.

When I returned to find them an hour later, the tree was barely visible behind a pile of ripped boxes and an ocean of yet more discarded gift-wrapping. The kids were entertaining themselves with a game of darts – one of the things Anna had bought for them. What an ideal gift for three youngsters, all under the age of ten! Perhaps she was hoping they would commit accidental harikiri with the sharp pointy ends?

With a sigh, I decided to make a half-hearted attempt to stuff the turkey and prepare the vegetables for lunch before taking on the mammoth task of tidying up. MDH had bought the kids a mobile phone each and I found battery covers, instructions and SIM cards strewn all over the place. My heart momentarily went out to him and his attempt to maintain contact with his kids, whilst giving them something they'd been hankering after for months.

Ten giant bin bags later, I'd cleared all the Christmas present detritus away. I made the kids sit down for breakfast and even managed to ensure they ate something. I had wanted to get them all bathed and dressed in their finery for Christmas lunch, but decided that was a hope too far. I still had so much to do including laying the table. I'd always taken real pains over this in the past, planning it for weeks. Normally my festive dinner table looked like something out of *Homes & Gardens*, but this year's Christmas theme seemed more akin to war-torn Iraq.

Finally, my tardy girlfriend appeared having showered and got all tarted up. Bugger me, it wasn't fair! She looked gorgeous, but all I really wanted to do was to hate her for being bloody useless when it came to lending a hand. Instead, I did what I always did – metaphorically licked her feet.

I smoked and drank my way through the rest of the lunch preparations like some female Keith Floyd. Once again, Anna had made herself scarce.

The kids picked up flying speed, thanks to gobfuls of brightly coloured sweets and a couple of Cadbury selection boxes apiece. Several toys had already been broken, including the dartboard, which hadn't gone unnoticed or unremarked upon by Anna. As lunchtime approached, I became increasingly sloshed and the kids' behaviour further deteriorated.

Having cocked up my timings, when I finally heaved the turkey out of the oven it had an air of a Hollywood has-been after yet another surgical procedure.

It was three o'clock by the time we sat down to eat. Well, when Anna and I sat down. The kids were up and down like fiddlers' elbows. Try as I might, I couldn't get them to sit still, or even stay in the same place. Dinner became like a nightmarish game of musical chairs punctuated by party poppers depositing thin paper streamers in everyone's plates of cold food.

Anna was seething. The kids were infuriating her. Whenever the opportunity presented itself she gave me one of her special looks accompanied by a swift nod of the head, which translated as 'keep your fucking brats under control'.

I suggested we all calm down and watch the family blockbuster on TV. I might as well have suggested we all stuff Christmas baubles up our bottoms from the reaction I got from Anna. The corners of her lips dropped even further and she pulled me into the hallway.

"This is the worst Christmas I've ever had ever. Your kids are spoilt little bastards and I am NOT spending any more time with them today. I am going to watch television in our room and, if you had any sense, you'd join me."

"Fuck you," I responded, full of Christmas spirits. "Perhaps if you'd been a proper partner and helped me through all this bedlam, it would have been easier for everyone. The kids' lives are in turmoil. Their parents are splitting up and their mother is with a woman. Can't you put yourself in their shoes for once?"

"Don't be stupid," she snarled. "In comparison to most children, they have a charmed life. They get everything they want, they go to private school, they live in a big house. They don't know they're born."

Here was another example of an unwinnable argument, the likes of which I would continue to have with Anna over the coming months. She found it impossible to empathise with anyone. To her, life focussed on material things and not a person's emotional well-being unless, of course, it was her own.

She trudged up the stairs, tripping over at the top and rather ruining her dramatic exit. I couldn't help chuckling, which only added to her scarlet-faced rage.

The kids and I snuggled up on the sofa and watched TV together. Later on, I made cold turkey sandwiches accompanied by endless bags of snacks. We warmed up mince pies and cut the Christmas cake we'd all decorated earlier in the week. Washed down with a bottle of my favourite Baileys, I found I was enjoying myself and the kids seemed to be considerably calmer. I even managed to get them all in the bath before bedtime, finishing the day with a story from one of their new books.

As I nervously climbed the stairs to the attic bedroom, I heard the familiar strains of the *Coronation Street* theme tune blaring from the television. Poking my head round the door, I could see Anna had fallen asleep. Next to her was an ashtray heaped with cigarette butts, plus an array of empty miniatures she must have brought with her.

I headed back downstairs and poured myself a large one. At that point, I didn't care what I drank as long as it WAS a large one.

I spent the last few hours of Christmas Day on my own. For some drunken reason, I lay underneath the Christmas tree looking up into the branches. In my inebriated state, the lights and all the sparkly decorations reminded me of being at the fairground when I was little. Surrounded by an assortment of bottles for company, my helter-skelter journey downwards into alcoholism picked up apace.

Everyone drinks. We live in a culture defined by alcohol. So it's easy to miss those tell tale signs that your own drinking is out of control. To be honest, you do everything you can to ignore them.

At one stage, I went to the doctor when MDH suggested my drinking had got out of hand. Rather than be diagnosed as a drunk, I convinced the poor man I was suffering from depression and had him prescribe me something for it. Much better than telling the truth.

The truth eh? Not something we drunks are good at. It starts with little lies in an attempt to conceal your drinking.

You begin to almost enjoy lying. It becomes second nature. You tell lies about anything. I've convinced strangers I was an airline pilot, a burlesque dancer, a TV chef and a leading heart surgeon before now. Just for the hell of it.

You take risks because you are invincible. You'll drive over the limit and not give a toss about whose lives you're endangering. Or hang out of the window at the top of a tall building or walk along railway lines or accept lifts from strangers.

Being desperate for a drink, no matter what time of day it is, is normal isn't it? Even if it means sneaking out of work, missing appointments as well as letting down friends and family. After all, if you don't know where your next drink is coming from, you'll panic and that's not good for anyone.

It's not long before you find yourself having to drink more as your tolerance to alcohol builds up. The only way to do this is by making sure you have access to booze at all times. Glove compartments, filing cabinets and the washing basket are all perfect hiding places for your liquid stash. And that's just the start.

CHAPTER 14

MDH returned from his travels just before New Year's Eve to spend his allotted time with the kids. So there it was. Another Christmas over and done with and ahead of me lay my first New Year's celebrations without my children. Heading out of London as I sat next to Anna, I realised how dreadful MDH must have felt, leaving them behind at Christmas.

As I grew increasingly silent with each passing mile, Anna seemed to come back to life. She held my hand most of the way back, chatted enthusiastically about what we'd do over the next couple of days including her plans to get me into bed. I smiled automatically. She seemed back to her old self again. I just felt old.

New Year came in with a dull thud and very little to report. All too quickly I was back at work. Having been the blue-eyed girl at HellFire, I'd become the black sheep of the company over the holidays. Someone, it transpired, had informed Tom that I was gay. As a fully signed-up member of the "Homophobic Testosterone-Fuelled Can't Keep My Trouser Snake Where It Belongs Society", this didn't go down too well. I suspected he'd had one of those changing room experiences at his terribly posh single sex public school, which he'd enjoyed a little too much.

Anyway, life became decidedly difficult. He moved my entire PR team up to a different floor and followed suit, taking pole position in the office. He watched my every move like a hawk and the 'hail fellow well met' attitude had switched to thinly disguised hatred.

Tom was a loud and bumptious man from the old school of advertising. Lunch was about entertaining clients with several bottles of jolly good red wine, whilst heartily slapping everyone on the back. Well oiled for an afternoon on the phone, his voice boomed across the room making it impossible to concentrate or talk to anyone.

If he wasn't schmoozing some potential client, he was playing table football with his retinue of oily advertising executives. It was totally overbearing and distracting, especially as I had a few big pitches to prepare.

When I originally joined the company, I distinctly remembered Tom telling me to treat the business like my own. In the past, when I had to focus on something important for work, I'd done it from home.

So I planned to do just that for a couple of days to get my various presentations finished without the whirr of spinning plastic footballers rattling through my head. As I was getting into my stride, the phone rang. It was Tom.

"Where the hell are you?"

"As I told my team, working from home to get these new business pitches finished."

"I think you should damned well do that at work like the rest of the management team seem able to do. Make sure you're back tomorrow."

The phone went dead and my hands clenched into tight little fists. I headed over to the drinks cabinet and grabbed the whisky bottle. I needed a coffee with a bit of a kick to it. Talking of kick, I would have happily planted my foot in Tom's fulsome backside at that very moment.

And so it continued. No matter what positive achievements the team and I made, there was always something not quite right. Great -

now I had a choice of mix-and-match stress stomachs - work and/or personal life. The only way I knew of dealing with all these feelings was to drown them in drink. I started having a liquid lunch on a daily basis. On the up side, my dress size went down to a 10.

I sniffed out whichever group from work were off to the pub and tagged along. Not that I socialised with them - just flung a few drinks down my neck before returning to the office. I became very familiar with the scores of watering holes all within a minute's stagger of HellFire.

Then, in February, a buyer for our house came along. Happy Valentine's! Now what?

MDH and I sat down for a serious talk about the future. Our business had folded and MDH, to his credit, had dealt with most of the fallout. Since then, he'd been on the job trail without much success. I knew why. "Why use one word when 100 will do?" was his motto. He bamboozled people with his speeches. It was Chinese takeaway conversation. After an awful lot of it, you still felt hungry for something more substantial.

We agreed neither of us were capable of giving the kids a stable home life at that moment in time. MDH had picked up on the fact that my relationship with Anna was not the hoped-for bed of roses. On top of that, it was hardly much of a secret that I was drinking heavily. Of course, I insisted my drinking was completely under control and never affected the kids. I actually believed everything I said, too. For his part, he was on supersize antidepressants and under the care of a 'team of top psychiatrists'. MDH could hardly look after himself, let alone three small children.

NO EARTH MOTHER, ME.

You don't know how you're going to respond when you're finally presented with that bundle of joy you've been carrying around for nine months. I was a bit nonplussed I have to admit. I always tackled the birthing part with extreme enthusiasm, but struggled with the bonding bit.

When my eldest was born, all the mothers on the ward commented on what a good baby he was. He slept most of the time and hardly cried. I was doing my best to breastfeed him, although it was proving to be toe curling, literally. Anyway, one of the nurses decided to do a blood test and discovered his blood sugar was so low, the poor little sod was nearly comatose. A bottle of formula was slapped in my hand following much tutting and head shaking.

The next day I was visited by a very odd little woman dead set on lecturing me about birth control. Strangely enough, it was not top of my list to discuss as I sat perched on an inflatable rubber ring to ease the unbelievable pain of birthing-induced piles. She also pointed out that my baby was lying next to his own sick. I asked her whether this was dangerous and was subjected to yet more tutting and head shaking.

At my National Childbirth Trust post-birthing get-together, I was also made to feel like a scarlet woman. When I asked the instructor whether she had a microwave to heat up a bottle for my son, she told me bottle-feeding was an abomination. She certainly wasn't going to offer assistance to anyone who wasn't breastfeeding. Hang on a minute lady! Not everyone is built like a prize-winning dairy cow, so stick your propaganda where the sun don't shine along with your spelt cakes for good measure.

We worked it out between us, my little baby boy and I. I fell head over heels in love with him and would have happily become a stay-at-home mum, but MDH had other plans of course.

Despite the fact our youngest was just seven, boarding school seemed the only option open to us. It would give our children a safe environment where they'd experience boundaries, discipline, continuity of care and somewhere free from conflict.

A few years previously, we'd looked at a lovely little school in the Cotswolds. At the time we'd been considering moving away from London and starting a new life in the country. As with most of our grand plans, it had come to nothing. We decided that this would be the perfect school for them, with the added benefit of being close to their grandparents.

Thankfully, we were able to get financial help from a charity for families in crisis, which made the school fees affordable. Although it was a heart-breaking decision for both of us, we knew our kids needed to be away from this maelstrom. It was up to us to put the best spin on it we could for their sakes. I tried my hardest to get them to read lots of rattling good yarns like Enid Blyton's *Claudine at St Clare's,* but they didn't seem too keen.

As completion day on the house drew nearer, we knew we'd have to get rid of a lot of the stuff we'd recklessly accumulated. MDH had found a small flat in Hackney, which was spatially challenged and my only option was to move in with Anna.

Once Anna found out the children were going to be safely installed in boarding school, she got very animated about the prospect of us living together. Actually, living together suggests an equal footing. In reality, it would turn out I would be living in Anna's house.

Firstly, there was the issue over our cats. I desperately wanted to keep them so the kids could see them during their holidays. Anna refused, point blank. I then suggested trying to find a home for them in her village, but I was blocked on this too. My parents couldn't have them, so after weeks of soul searching, we found a good home for them with complete strangers. The kids never saw their 'pussy cats' ever again.

Next we discussed my furniture. It wasn't as if I wanted to bring vast antique armoires with me. In fact, all it amounted to was an old Chinese table that had belonged to my grandmother plus a couple of my favourite pictures. Anna explained there simply wasn't room. What's more, our taste in art was completely different and she didn't like mine. Instead of standing my ground, I meekly went along with her decision.

So I told MDH he could keep any of the furniture he liked. Beyond that, anything worth hanging on to would go into storage and, when I found a place of my own, I would take out whatever I needed. It was with a sinking heart that I realised the relationship I was leaving behind was morphing into something more adult than the one I was now getting deeper into.

A lot of our things ended up in a huge skip that sat on the road outside our house for weeks. Had we been better organised, we could have made a killing at a car boot sale.

I soon discovered that a night-time visit to our skip for a quick pilfer had become 'all the rage' in the neighbourhood. We would fill it up in the daytime and, as dusk descended, shadowy figures would approach to have a good rummage through our cast offs.

We threw away clothes, endless toys and games, books, kitchenware and tools, most of which were virtually brand new.

A lot of it found its way to new and appreciative homes. It was rather like a covert charity shop, but all free and without any sense of charity.

As well as my home life being dismantled, work continued to fall apart. I was always being admonished for something or another and the whole business of going into work had become truly depressing. Had it not been for the project I was working on with the events team at HellFire – who all thought I was shit hot – my self-esteem would have been as low as a dachshund's scrotum.

It was a joint campaign to launch a new chain of adult stores across the UK – the first being in Soho, unsurprisingly.

The party to mark the London store revolved around giant chocolate fountains and Page 3 glamour girls. I'd done the best I could to get all the red top media to attend but, at the end of the day, it really didn't matter. The CEO was more interested in turning it into a private party for a few hundred of his closest friends.

I'd pleaded with Anna to come along and join me for the evening. I was being put up in a rather nice hotel and thought it would be a real treat for both of us. She had played her usual non-committal card, but on the day itself uttered something about trying to get there for around seven. So instead of being entirely focussed on proceedings, I was constantly scanning the crowd to see if I could spot Anna.

Seven o'clock came and went with no sign of her. Neither had she sent me a text or left a phone message. I tried ringing her at home, but it was on answer-phone so I assumed she was on her way and stuck in traffic.

Despite the fact the champagne was flowing liberally, I managed to avoid drinking a single drop. I wanted to be completely sober when Anna arrived and prove to her what a good girl I could be. To keep myself occupied, I hung out behind the chocolate fountains and tried every conceivable combination of food items that could be dipped in plain, milk or white chocolate. To keep ennui at bay, I experimented with things not really intended for the chocolate fountain. Well, it was a sex shop and playful fun is meant to be a big part of foreplay isn't it?

As the night wore on, a sick sensation gripped my stomach. I couldn't decide whether it was overindulgence on the chocolate front or the growing realisation that Anna was going to be a no show. The store launch party came to a close and everyone moved on to some posh club to continue the forced jollity.

Reluctantly I followed the crowd the short distance to the venue. The place was already full of scantily clad women and some Z-list celebrities.

One of the top executives at HellFire tottered across the dance floor to where I was standing with one of the younger members of my team. He was brandishing a bag of white powder and thrust it at us. Now, I like my drink, it has to be said, but I've always drawn the line at cocaine.

Fiona, my junior executive, had only just left home and an over-protected childhood in the wilds of Scotland. She looked completely stunned and disappeared to the loo crying. An evening of sex and drugs was proving all too much for her.

As there was little for the PR team to do at the club, I told Fiona to go home. I decided to call it a night as well. We all had to be up early the next morning to deliver aphrodisiac breakfasts to the City's radio stations as the final part of the campaign.

When I got back to the hotel room, I was hoping Anna might have decided to make her way there to surprise me. I was bitterly disappointed she'd not made the effort to attend something I'd had a big part in organising. I'd had to tag along to several of her industry extravaganzas, which had all been a complete yawn.

I tried her phone again and this time she answered. Apparently she'd been to the gym.

"So why didn't you let me know you weren't coming?" I asked.

"As a test."

"A test of what?"

"To see whether you'd drink and whether you'd behave yourself in my absence. So, well done, darling – you passed."

Keeping cool, calm and collected even though I was raging inside, I told her how pissed off I was. She hardly paid lip service to my anger and didn't even bother to ask how it had all gone. She was more interested in telling me about her own work and some dull story that revolved around missing paperwork for one of her clients. I lost interest and scrolled through the hotel's film menu searching for something to match my hack and slash mood.

When I put the phone down, I dived into the minibar. Emptying its entire contents – except the soft drink options – I lined the miniatures along the bed. A small army of soldiers coming to my rescue. I knocked each of them back in a single gulp and fell into an uncomfortable sleep well before the film had ended.

Hours later, I was disturbed from my slumbers by the bedside phone jangling in my ear. It was Fiona who was already at the office and wondering where on earth I was.

"Tom's looking for you," she whispered.

"What the blazes is he doing in so early?"

"His wife is the one doing the catering for our breakfasts, remember, so he came in with her."

"Bugger, bugger, bugger. Tell him I had to pop out for some cigarettes or something."

"OK, but try to get here as quickly as you can. We need to head out in about 20 minutes."

"Will do."

Jesus, how crap was that? A girl barely out of nappies telling her hungover and tardy boss to get a move on.

I hastily got dressed. There wasn't even time for a shower. To save the bother of bringing an overnight bag with me, I'd decided to recycle the clothes from the previous night. It was not a good idea in retrospect. Everything was crumpled, stank of smoke and there was a large red wine stain in an unfortunate place on my skirt that I'd not spotted last night. Trying to run in ridiculously high heels was also proving impossible. One of them got caught in some grating and I found myself sprawled on the pavement in the middle of Oxford Street.

My linen suit was now smudged with dirt and the offending heel had completely snapped off. I managed to dislodge it and stuck it in my handbag. I continued to make my way with a 'Monty Python's Ministry of Funny Walks' gait.

By the time I got to the office, Fiona had already left in the taxi. I headed to the art department and found something that looked like superglue, which I used to quickly mend my shoe.

As I hobbled to my desk, I noticed Tom was already in situ and glaring, red faced, at me.

"Good night last night?" he enquired with a hint of sarcasm.

"It all seemed to go pretty well, yes."

"So why didn't you stay at the club, then?"

"It was midnight by the time we all got there. There wasn't really anything I could do and the media had gone home well before that. Is there a problem?"

"I would have expected a senior member of the management team like yourself to stay to the bitter end to oversee things and take care of the client."

At that very moment, the make-do-and-mend on my shoe came unstuck with a sudden snap and I found myself facing Tom at a rather odd angle. The heel had somehow managed to ping across the room and embed itself in Tom's wastepaper basket. He first looked at me and then at my heel like we were the worst form of pond life.

Desperate to divert attention from myself, I straightened up and became the lowest of the low – a snitch.

"And I would have expected executives more senior than myself not to go around offering office juniors drugs as if they were sweeties."

"What are you talking about?"

I went through the previous night's events, laying it on with a trowel – especially the bit about Fiona's tears. I knew I was limping on slightly thin ice. I had heard, on the office grapevine, that Tom, as well as most of the other directors, often asked junior members of staff to supply them with all sorts of illegal goodies in advance of their big nights out.

Nevertheless, I had managed to temporarily extract myself from the focus of things and headed off to the kitchen to make a strong coffee. Tom disappeared in the opposite direction, mumbling obscenities under his breath.

I knew my days at Hellfire were distinctly numbered.

CHAPTER 15

Amidst all the on-going to-do at work, the house sale was progressing rapidly. Easter was approaching and the kids were due to start at their new school in the summer term.

MDH wanted to spend Easter following some bike race in Flanders. As my parents were going away, I decided to decamp to their house for the holiday and spend it on my own with the kids. I thought it might be a little melancholy to stay at home, given it would be the last big celebration we'd all share under that particular roof.

Anna was going across to see her mother in Norfolk and I felt like I was still 'persona non grata' in that neck of the woods after the Christmas fiasco.

We spent Easter following simple pursuits. Visiting a local farm to bottle feed lambs, walking on the hills and taking part in endless Easter egg hunts – always the highlight of Easter holidays for my children.

There, I managed to paint a picture of pastoral perfection for you, didn't I? A veritable double-page spread from *Good Housekeeping* about how 'one' should organise a traditional Easter for 'one's' family.

In fairness, we did do a lot of those things, but I also drove the kids down to the local pub at opening time every morning. Having bought endless bottles of Coca-Cola and an assortment of interesting snacks, I would sit and watch them play pool whilst I enjoyed pint after pint of local cider. The amount I drank would depend on whether I'd heard from Anna that morning or how our conversation the previous evening had panned out.

After an hour or so at the pub, I'd pile the kids into the people mover and take a convoluted route to our next destination. This involved a complex network of country lanes to avoid being spotted by the police. A couple of hours later, we'd probably find another watering hole so I could top up my alcohol levels.

I'd buy the kids some kind of takeaway for tea. Back at the house, I'd set the kids up in front of the video with a pile of sweets and carbonated drinks. Then I'd mix myself a few cocktails and sit out on the terrace whilst smoking the best part of a packet of cigarettes. Anna would either ring me after she and her mother had finished watching the soaps or later, when they had got back from the pub.

My goal was to get the kids to bed as early as possible so I had plenty of time to myself to drink each evening. It didn't matter what I drank. One night I had about two-dozen snowballs when I discovered some bottles of advocaat in my parents' garage. I've never had a problem helping myself to other people's booze without permission.

OTHER PEOPLE'S BOOZE

My earliest help-yourself memory harks back to the time I was left at the cleaner's house for the day whilst my parents were both at work. I must have been about four. I found myself sitting next to a sideboard full of interesting knick-knacks and bottles of liqueurs from all over the globe. I took a world tour. Having taken little sips from each of them, I discovered a particular penchant for cherry brandy. I was flat out when my mum came to collect me and no one could work out why.

Growing up, I would sneak a sip of sherry from the glasses of guests attending the endless drinks parties my parents seemed to have. Sometimes I'd even go straight for the decanter and use a straw.

Aged sixteen, at someone's house party and pissed as a hand-cart, a friend and I fell backwards into a walk-in wardrobe. As luck would have it, we landed on several bottles of vintage claret that the parents of the house had hidden away. Not carefully enough as it turned out. Without a hint of conscience, we opened all of the bottles, took a few sips from each and then used the bottles, still half full, as the most expensive ash-trays known to man.

The world becomes your prairie oyster. It's quite easy to have a few slugs from someone else's glass without being noticed whilst you're waiting at a crowded bar – even if you are spotted, a winning smile usually gets you off the hook.

Then there's minesweeping (refer back to the chapter about my first weekend at Anna's) – a great way to continue drinking even after the bar has closed. As an alcoholic, I could never understand how anyone could leave a glass, which still had something in it. I would always wring out the very last drop.

Back in London, our final night at home arrived with a deathly inevitability. We spent the day getting the children packed up as best we could. Now that we were officially charity cases, even their school uniforms were to be provided free of charge. A mix of second-hand items and lost property as it turned out.

The kids and I had been through the soul-destroying task of choosing a few of their favourite toys as they were only allowed to take a handful of things with them. Clothes too, had been whittled down to the necessities, as the school stipulated that home clothes were only to be worn at the weekend.

With the children asleep, I wandered to and from their bedrooms, weeping my heart out over the bloody mess I'd created. It all felt so unreal and the thought of living with Anna 24/7 didn't fill me with the joy I had imagined it would when I'd first met her. In fact, I felt plain scared.

MDH was in no better shape. From tomorrow, he would be living in the house alone until the contracts were finally signed. I didn't envy him the prospect of meeting the ghosts of bygone times in every room and on each stair. I did my best to scout around the place to remove anything that could stir up memories for him – a baby sock fallen behind a radiator, a couple of sorry-looking footballs in the garden, Yu-Gi-Oh cards that had slipped under a mat.

When the morning came, we decided to go for a family breakfast at a one-time favourite haunt of ours. It was a little Italian café in Teddington – big on fry-ups but not so big on healthy eating. It was always filled with the local nipperati. That morning most of the food seemed to catch in my throat. Everyone was subdued and even the geniality of the large chef couldn't put a smile on the kids' faces. He always handed out lollipops at the end of a meal, which were usually the highlight of the visit. This time they were left on the table, unwrapped and completely forgotten about.

We finished packing up the cars. MDH was going to head up our sorry little convoy, driving the kids in the people mover. I was to follow behind in a clapped-out old Volvo my uncle had kindly lent me for the time being. I drove up the M40 with my entire life crammed into a selection of bin bags and cases. I'd pared it down to clothes and toiletries following the edict issued by Anna. I'd given up trying to argue my corner over my belongings by then.

Our drive up to the Cotswolds seemed to take forever. It was one of those featureless days when just looking at the sky could bring on a headache. The route was busy with Sunday traffic. The drone of passing cars grated on my nerves. I desperately needed a drink but really didn't want to turn up at the school smelling of booze. Well, not on this occasion.

Neither MDH nor I had realised how swift the kids' entrenchment into their new institution would be. The short, sharp, shock treatment was deliberately meant to lessen the anguish for both parents and children but it felt brutal. Within minutes of arriving, our children had been escorted to their various dormitories and, after a lukewarm reception and a cup of tea, we were shown the door.

MDH and I stood outside on the pavement looking at each other. Neither of us knew what to say or do and we felt like lost children ourselves.

"Well, goodbye, then," I said, giving MDH a hug. He clung onto me as if I were the last remaining shred of his comfort blanket.

"Goodbye. Good luck with your new living arrangements. I really mean that."

"I hope your place works out too. I'll come down and help on the day you actually move out, like I promised."

"Yep, that would be good."

"And we both know the kids are safer here for the time being. We're both a bit damaged to be much use to them right now."

"I know and they'll have a great time. Just see it as the end of another chapter."

It didn't feel as if we'd done a very good job of convincing ourselves this was the right thing. But it was.

With that MDH turned and walked away. I knew he was crying and for the first time, I realised that this whole affair had truly devastated him. I suddenly threw up, managing to target the gutter. I cast a swift glance over my shoulder to make sure no one had been watching me. The windows of the school were empty and MDH was all but a shadow in the distance.

I headed into the nearby town and drove around until I found a shop that was open. Medicinal brandy was required. I sat in the supermarket car park and took a few gulps before I decided to ring Anna.

"Hi, sweetheart, I'm on my way. I feel awful."

"What's wrong?" Anna asked, sounding almost genuine.

"I just feel so sad leaving the kids," I replied.

The brief pause before she spoke made it clear I'd said the wrong thing.

"Well, why not turn around and go back to them if that's the way you feel?" she taunted, every ounce of concern gone from her voice.

"Oh, don't be so foolish. You have no idea what all this is like."

"No, you're right, I don't. Why not call my mother? I am sure she'll be able to provide a shoulder to cry on. So let me know if you're held up in traffic – if you're still coming, that is."

With that, she put the phone down. Yet again I was overwhelmed with an aching sense of loneliness. I drank the rest of the brandy as if it were a bottle of pop. It did nothing to lift my spirits. Slowly, I drove away from the place where I felt I'd left the better part of my heart and headed towards my new life with Anna.

I knew Anna was cross that I wasn't more upbeat about moving in with her. She found it impossible to relate to any of the feelings I had for my children. The more time you spend with a person, the more you slowly discover about them until you reach their core. Their soul, I suppose. With Anna, no matter how many layers I pulled back, I never seemed to get anywhere. Would I ever discover her soul? Did she even have one or was there just a gaping hole where it was supposed to be?

With the radio blaring, I tried to feel more positive about things. Even the sun came out as I drove the final few miles along the country lanes leading to Anna's village.

She was waiting for me on the doorstep. She helped me haul my bags in before ushering me upstairs to the main bathroom. This was to be the one I was to use from now on. She didn't want me to share the en suite, as she was "a bit funny about other people's dirt".

Anna had been out and bought a set of cheap metal drawers from Argos for me to put all my cosmetics in. From the way she demonstrated it to me, you'd have thought it was something she'd handcrafted from a single piece of rare jade. I managed to convince her that I was thrilled.

Downstairs she opened up kitchen cupboards and her fridge to show me the food she had stockpiled from Lidl. She seemed childishly happy and my heart melted a bit. It seemed like Anna was really trying.

The next couple of hours I spent unpacking my things. Anna's bedroom wardrobes were already heaving with her clothes, although she rarely wore any of them. She'd even converted her smallest bedroom into a walk-in cupboard exclusively for all her shoes. Imelda Marcos, eat your heart out. This meant my stuff had to be squeezed into a small wardrobe in the spare bedroom. I also had the use of a couple of drawers in an equally small chest.

The view from the spare room was pretty. The house was at the edge of the village beyond which were endless fields filled with sheep contentedly grazing. It was the sort of image Americans conjure up when they think of England. Despite this bucolic idyll, I was still feeling empty and emotionally weary. Tomorrow was the start of my life as a long-distance commuter. I needed to be up at five a.m. in order to be at my desk for nine. The train from Peterborough was direct but then

I had to enter the bowels of London's underground to reach my final destination. It wasn't a journey I was relishing one bit.

CHAPTER 16

For the first week or so, Anna got up at the same time as I did to make me a packed lunch to take to work. When I say packed lunch, it was more like a crammed lunch as there was so much food involved. Half a loaf of bread masquerading as sandwiches, an entire packet of chocolate biscuits, handfuls of sweets, savoury scones – you name it, in it went.

If I had gorged myself on this daily carrier bag of scoff, I would have ballooned up like the Pillsbury Doughboy. As it was, I scattered the contents out of my car window en route to Peterborough Station. I imagined the Lincolnshire wildlife lining the country lanes waiting excitedly for their daily booty. I always made certain to memorise the contents down to the last crumb, as Anna was prone to quizzing me most evenings.

The daily commute was as hateful as I had imagined it would be. I got into the habit of buying a large latte with vanilla syrup to take with me on the train – the highlight of my morning. Actually, it was often the highlight of my entire day.

Now that I was living with Anna, she took complete ownership of me and I began to feel like a pet. She would call me several times a day to check on my whereabouts. If I didn't respond to her emails or answer my phone, she would become manic and call any member of my office team in her attempt to track me down. At first I was flattered, but it soon became embarrassing and then downright irritating.

She also demanded that I leave work bang on five thirty p.m. so that we "had our evenings together". I tried to explain that creative businesses didn't work like that, but it was pointless. So, I'd be the first to leave at night, which didn't further endear me to Tom.

One evening, we'd gone out to the pub in the next village that did "posh food". Propping up the bar was Arthur who I'd not really seen since our first memorable meeting. Apparently he kept the pub supplied with venison, pheasant and any other spoils he purloined on his rounds. In return, the pub provided him with all the drink and food he could consume, which seemed to be a great deal judging by the circumference of his girth.

Anna and Arthur began to reminisce about the good old days. I was surprised at the amount of socialising they'd done together despite being a bizarre and ill-matched couple.

Talk turned to yet another pub in yet another neighbouring village and yet another night the pair of them had spent sampling the local ale.

"Do you remember the cat incident?" Anna asked Arthur.

He chuckled and took another swig of his beer.

"Went up like kindling," he responded.

"What?" I asked, sensing that I wasn't going to like what I was about to hear.

Anna took up the story putting me in mind of those cheerful narrators on children's television.

"Arthur and the landlady of this pub had been having a bit of a to-do about something or other. Anyway, her blasted cat had been bothering us all night, winding in and out of our legs, you know how cats do."

She smiled to herself, then made eye contact with me as if to establish whether I was ready for the punch line.

"So Arthur here leant down and set fire to the tip of the cat's tail with his Zippo. Looked like a firebrand. It certainly left us alone after that."

I couldn't believe what I'd just heard and sat in stunned silence. Both of them looked at me. They seemed surprised not to get an immediate and more enthusiastic response to their psychopathic tale. What were they hoping for? A round of applause, a slap on the back and much guffawing?

"Was the cat all right?" I asked.

Neither of them knew the answer and that wasn't the point of the story, they told me. Having not got the hoped-for reaction, their conversation turned to some World War II truck that Arthur was in the process of restoring. No doubt plans for that included the addition of bull bars to ram local wildlife or perhaps any small child that got in his way?

Still in a catatonic state, I ordered another round of drinks, making sure mine was a double, and sat in silence for the rest of the evening.

Anna was furious with me when we got in the car.

"How could you be so rude? Arthur's a good friend of mine. I was so embarrassed. You hardly said a word all night!"

"What? I was horrified - that poor cat. How could he treat an animal like that and how could you condone it?"

"There you go, using long words again. It was only a cat, for God's sake, and it's none of your business anyway."

"You're kidding me?"

"It's different in the country. Killing animals is a way of life. Everyone goes hunting and fishing."

"Oh, so it did die, you're saying?"

I was certain setting fire to cats had not yet become an acceptable country pursuit.

I lay in bed that night, thinking about the cat and wondering whether it had survived. It continued to trouble me the following day too. When I got home from work that evening, I was astonished to find that Anna had been out and bought a rabbit and a guinea pig.

Her intention, I'm certain, was to prove that I had got her all wrong and that she was, at heart, an animal lover. As it happened, I have a complete aversion to guinea pigs as they remind me of my unhappy days at school.

UNHAPPY DAYS AT SCHOOL

A lovely teacher at my junior school bought us a guinea pig as a class pet. Unfortunately, I didn't bond with it as I found all the squeaking and hiding under straw a little bit boring. So I was hardly filled with delight when my name was drawn out of the hat to be the first to take it home over the Christmas holidays. Hallelujah!

Anyway I did my best to look after it. I fed it and cleaned it out. So imagine my horror when I came down one morning to find it stiff as a board. It was as dead as dead could be. Neither was I Little Miss Popular with my classmates when I had to admit to the terrible truth at the start of the term. I'd not hidden my feelings for the blessed creature so everybody assumed I'd deliberately done away with it. Guinea Pig Slayer.

So Anna took the guinea pig back to the pet shop the next day and lavished all her attention on the rabbit. Her focus began to shift away from me. The packed lunches soon stopped as she was too busy first thing scouring the hedgerows for tasty morsels for the imaginatively named Bugsy. It was a huge relief for me, but I think the woodland creatures of Lincolnshire were a little disappointed not to get their daily rations.

Bugsy soon became a house rabbit and had the run of the sitting room every night, crapping and nibbling wherever and whenever to his heart's content. Electrical items stopped working and the cause, inevitably, was a chewed wire. A pile of droppings provided the evidence that the darned rabbit had been at work.

I pointed out to Anna that, for someone who retched at the mere mention of a cat litter tray, it was a little hypocritical to allow a rabbit free rein with his bowels. Of course this led to one of our major altercations and I ended up locked in my bathroom, sobbing. I had found the perfect hiding place behind the hot water tank in the airing cupboard to stow my supplies of alcohol. As well as bringing back a bottle of plonk or a couple of cans of lager in my briefcase most days, I'd 'disappeared' a few bottles of spirits from Anna's drinks cabinet too. I had put together an impressive a collection, which was fortunate as I was finding the need to turn to the bottle most evenings.

I anaesthetised myself to the point I no longer cared whether Anna was angry with me or not. Whatever she said or did, I let her get away with it. If she stepped over a boundary, I just redrew the boundary. Anything to accommodate this woman I loved with the unquestioning loyalty of a rescue dog.

As I was leaving for work the next day, she looked me up and down with disdain and told me the outfit I was wearing made me look like a slut. Apparently, I was showing too much cleavage. Given I was a modest 36A and hardly built on the scale of Marilyn Monroe, this was verging on hyperbole. But I dutifully put on something she felt more appropriate and headed off with a high neckline and a low morale.

Will, my friend on the events team at Hellfire, picked up on my world weariness the moment I shuffled in to work and offered to take me out for lunch to cheer me up. Of course, mine ended up being of the liquid variety.

I was not a comfort eater, more of a comfort starver. I chose alcohol over food every time and was more than happy to let Will tuck into a massive BLT and chips whilst I downed a bottle of rosé.

Still trying to maintain a façade that all was well between Anna and myself, I waxed lyrical about how deeply in love I was. Sadly, this was the truth. The mistake I then made was to ring Anna in a moment of pissed loved-upness.

"I love you, darling, I really love you," I drawled.

"You've been drinking, haven't you?" I heard her exhale loudly.

"No, don't be silly. Here, speak to Will; we're having lunch."

Will nervously took the phone that I thrust at him.

"Hello… hello."

He made a face, which I knew meant Anna had maintained radio silence on the other end. I grabbed the phone off him and began burbling again.

"I really, really love…"

The phone went dead. Bollocks. I was going to be even deeper in the shit now. Anna hated being faced with the reality that I interacted with other people on a daily basis. Everyone was a potential threat in her eyes, especially when I was under the influence.

Oh well, in for a penny, in for a pound. There were times when I could drink anything and it had very little effect. This was not one of them. Will and I ordered a second bottle of rosé although I drank most of it… again. We then decided to celebrate our miserable lives with port and cigars, which we thought was hilarious.

Wandering back to work, the fresh air seemed to increase my inebriated state. I could barely walk, let alone maintain a straight line. Will suggested I go straight home offering to cover for me at work. I refused. I was infused with that superhuman confidence only drunks know.

I fell out of the lift when it opened on my level. Tom was standing there almost as if he had been waiting for me.

"Hello, Tomster," I slurred.

Tom was always adding 'ster' or 'meister' on to everyone's name, which I felt sure was his way of belittling people. He knew I was taking the piss.

"You're drunk," he growled.

Thinking I was being highly amusing, I grappled for a famous quote of Winston Churchill's:

"And you, sir, are butt ugly, but I won't be drunk tomorrow."

The delivery wasn't quite so eloquent as Churchill's, but the general gist remained the same. Tom was about to give me a piece of his mind, but I wasn't planning on hanging around to hear it. Off I stumbled in the general direction of my desk and fell into my seat shouting "Tomster's a knob!" at the top of my voice.

One of my team rushed off to make me a coffee, but no one was going to be able to contain me that day. I was on a 'ten reasons for your boss to fire you' mission.

My next brilliant idea was to lean against the football table and pretend to be Tom. Actually, it was a near-perfect impression having practised his irritating mannerisms on many occasions with Will. I was aware that people were stifling sniggers so I continued playing to the crowd.

I was interrupted by a colleague who whispered in my ear that the directors had demanded I meet with them in the boardroom – now. Although I was tempted to take up their offer and deliver an incoherent stream of abuse, I decided to quit whilst I was ahead.

Gathering my belongings, I headed out to the fire escape and made a furtive exit from the building for the day.

I ricocheted my way up to Oxford Circus Tube, pinging off people like an out-of-control pinball. By now the bravado had started to wear off and I was feeling queasy. I stood in the Tube station reeling and desperately trying to remember which train line I needed to take to get to King's Cross. I had a vague idea it was one of the blue ones.

Standing at the top of the escalator, I was gripped by an urge to throw myself on top of the descending crowd and cause a domino effect. I resisted the temptation but the thought made me giggle like a naughty schoolgirl.

It was at this point I had my first ever blackout. I have no recall of finding my way down to the platform or getting onto the train.

When I came to, I was lying on the station platform propped up against the wall. Much to my surprise, I was no longer at Oxford Circus but Seven Sisters – the station at the very end of the line. People were leaning over me with concerned faces. People in uniform. Police and ambulance-type people.

They initially thought I'd had some kind of fit. After all, I was a smartly dressed, middle-aged woman with a briefcase, so the thought I was 'three sheets to the wind' hadn't crossed their minds.

At that point, I blacked out again.

The next time I woke up, I was in hospital, in a curtained-off area of A&E. By now they had sussed out I was simply blotto and that there was no clear and present danger. I'd pretty much been abandoned by the staff to sober up whilst they dealt with real patients.

Thankfully, I had not lost my handbag during all the kerfuffle. I scrambled around for my mobile. Anna wasn't answering either phone. Not in the mood for game playing, and still with enough Dutch courage on board, I left her a venomous message.

I decided to try MDH. At least he answered. However, he already had plans and gave me umpteen reasons why he was unable to fetch me. Numerous phone calls later, I had still not found anyone to help me out of this latest problem.

Flagging down one of the nurses as she scuttled past, I asked if I could leave. I was told I'd have to wait until a doctor was available to discharge me. Bugger that for a game of soldiers. With a furtive glance, I stole out into the night. Now what?

I have no idea what possessed me but I found myself walking over to the taxi rank, where a line of private cabs were waiting. Without giving a second thought to my safety, I leapt into one of them – the driver turned around to ask me where I was heading.

I burst into tears explaining that I only had thirty pounds on me and just a month to live! My elderly mother was in Lincolnshire, I had just been diagnosed with terminal cancer and needed to inform her of my terrible news. Miraculously, the poor man believed every word and dutifully got out his map to plan the four-hour round trip. He didn't even quibble over the pitiful fare I'd offered.

On the way, I occupied myself by ringing anyone who'd listen to me badmouthing Anna, including Mavis. From her reaction, it was obvious I was not the first disenchanted lover to give her an earful about her daughter. She did her best to reassure me and promised to ring ahead and make sure Anna took good care of me when I got home. How did such a sweet little lady end up giving birth to the Devil's spawn?

My delightful taxi driver dropped me at the end of the lane as instructed. I was certain Anna would be in bed by now and I didn't want the sound of the taxi waking her. I planned to silently let myself in, and sleep on the living room sofa.

Unfortunately, as I fumbled noisily with my keys, the door opened as if by magic to reveal Anna. She was doing that annoying thing with her eyebrow again.

At that point in time, I had no energy left to do anything, let alone engage in unpleasant banter. Instead I gave her a peck on the cheek and scrambled upstairs to collapse into bed.

I came to abruptly the next day courtesy of Anna poking her bony finger in my ribs. Throwing open the curtains, she announced it was time to get up. With my tongue stuck to the roof of my mouth and my head pounding like the relentless road works on the A1, work was out of the question.

"I'm not going," I mumbled, pulling the duvet Anna had wrenched from my grasp back around me.

"Well, I'll call Tom and let him know exactly the reason you won't be in today then, shall I?"

"Go ahead, it won't take a degree in astrophysics for him to work that one out."

Memories of yesterday's performance at work came trickling back and I experienced that awful hot-under-the-collar sensation. Anna could see that I wasn't going anywhere and flounced out of the room and back to her office.

Before going back to sleep, I heard her muffled voice on the phone and assumed she was making a business call. True to her word, I later discovered Anna had rung Tom to fill him in on my missing hours since hotfooting it from the office yesterday. Were there no depths she wouldn't plumb to exact revenge whenever she felt slighted?

CHAPTER 17

Travelling to the office two days after my outburst, I was filled with a strange sense of excitement. I knew exactly what was going to happen and it would be a blessed relief. The only thing that was bothering me was money. MDH and I had made next to nothing on the house sale and my wafer-thin cushion of savings was now well worn. If they were going to fire me, surely they would need to give me some kind of financial compensation?

Anna was anal about equally splitting costs for everything including any shopping, the mortgage and all the household bills. I had no idea whether she'd help me out if I found myself penniless. She seemed quite capable of turning me out onto the streets or keeping a tally until I started earning again.

Tom called me the moment I sat down at my desk. I could almost hear him panting with excitement at the prospect of making me squirm. He was like a schoolboy filled with anticipation at the thought of pulling the wings off a fly.

"Come to the board room, will you?"

"Of course, Tom."

I was expecting to be met by several directors but Tom was on his own. I smiled at him, closing the door behind me.

"We've got to the point where we can no longer tolerate your behaviour. The day before yesterday you got stupidly drunk during office hours and caused mayhem."

"I agree, Tom. I can only apologise for the things I did and the things I said. I'm not dealing with life particularly well at the moment. Wrong time and wrong place, I suppose".

Tom looked crestfallen. I think he'd been hoping for a bit of a fight. I later learnt, via Will, that it was all he could do to stop himself from punching me, apparently adding 'that's all lesbians are good for'. Nice chap.

Having bargained with him over the terms of my dismissal, I hurried back to my desk, packed my things as hastily as I could, said a few hurried goodbyes and left the building. Tom had agreed that I could work out my last month from 'home'.

When I rang Anna to tell her the news, she sounded delighted. She told me I could now start my own business. Once it was established, she'd give up her job so that we could run the business together. Had that been her objective all along, I wondered? Nevertheless, it seemed the most sensible plan. My experience at HellFire had taught me that working for someone else was not for me. Neither was I cut out for commuting.

Anna threw herself at me when I arrived home. She was fuming about the way Tom had treated me. I thought better of pointing out that her two-penneth worth to Tom had hardly helped the situation. She'd already decided to turn the conservatory into my office. She'd ordered a couple of desks so she could work alongside me from time to time. Anna seemed genuinely pleased about things and was being sweeter than she had for a while.

That night we headed out for dinner – Anna's treat – to celebrate the start of 'our' new career. She'd chosen a very upmarket restaurant and, as I sat looking at her, the wine and the candlelight worked its magic. My heart ached for her and I prayed that, perhaps this time, we could get on with our new life together without any further upsets.

I hadn't felt so happy for a long time. I remember laughing a lot that night. Towards the end of the evening, Anna brought up the subject of the summer holidays, which were fast approaching.

"Why don't we take the kids to Norfolk for a week and have a traditional bucket-and-spade holiday?"

"Sounds idyllic – have you somewhere in mind?"

"There's a seaside town called Wells, which has loads of great things for all of us to do. I could take them crabbing?"

"Or we could head down to Cornwall?"

Anna pouted and I knew she'd already made up her mind.

Then came the bombshell. She'd decided the house was too small to accommodate everyone for an entire month. Besides the lack of space, there was the noise to consider, especially since both of us would now be working from home during the day.

"I could find a local summer camp or somewhere for them to go to in the daytime?" I suggested.

"I think you should find a place to rent for the four of you," she said as she gesticulated to the waiter for the bill.

Case dismissed.

Despite the fact I was now paying half towards everything, that it was now my home too and it wasn't that long ago she'd agreed the children would spend their holidays there, I went along with everything she suggested. She still had total control over me.

As far as work was concerned, I lost no time in approaching companies in the area and began rustling up new business. I had a knack of getting a foot in the door, so it didn't take long before I had half a dozen introductory meetings.

Within a fortnight, I'd got two clients signed up and enough of a monthly income to more than pay my way. I was going to need it as Anna had announced she expected me to continue paying my half of the mortgage whilst also renting a place for the kids over the summer.

The week of our trip to Norfolk arrived. I went to collect everyone at the end of term and put in an appearance at prize giving and sports day. On the way to East Anglia, we stopped at Lidl and loaded up the car with a week's shopping.

When we arrived in Wells, I got a text from Anna to say she was running late. I became hot and bothered in the process of unpacking everything as well as increasingly annoyed that Anna had left me with all the hard work as usual.

I took the kids to the nearest pub. Ensconced at an outside table with a large G&T, I watched them happily run around in the play area whilst awaiting Anna's arrival.

When she finally did turn up at our holiday property, I noticed she'd brought Bugsy with her. What on earth was she thinking?

"I thought the kids would enjoy having Bugsy around", she explained as she unloaded his hutch from the boot of her car.

My daughter was particularly excited about this addition to our family. She immediately asked if she could hold the rabbit and Anna's expression changed in a flash. She gave me her 'get that kid out of my face now' look. Good grief, did she think children were happy just to be spectators when it came to small furry animals?

Once we'd all helped Anna in with her stuff, we decided to explore Wells. The kids were keen to get hold of the things they needed to go crabbing – an activity which Anna had wittered on about non-stop since her arrival.

On the sea front we found a shop selling exactly what we were looking for – lines and bait, together with a large bucket for collecting the crabs. We were soon settled on the pier – Anna helping each of the kids to set up their crabbing line whilst I looked on proudly.

On the way home, we bought fish and chips for tea. The kids tugged on Anna's arms begging her to help them plan my birthday, which was the day after next.

MY BIRTHDAY LAST YEAR

I vividly remembered last year's birthday – it was not long after meeting Anna. The plan had been to spend the night in some romantic little hideaway.

However, the kibosh was put on all this when Anna announced she had long since arranged to have a facelift and her surgery had finally been scheduled to take place three days before my birthday. Apparently it was something she had promised herself when she turned fifty.

I was staggered. I was already convinced she was a distant cousin of Dorian Gray. She certainly didn't look her age. As well as not an ounce of spare fat on her, unlike some of her peers, she hadn't the slightest hint of a jowl or scraggy neck. Why did she need a facelift? But she was adamant.

I agreed to go over to her place instead. When I got there, the bride of Frankenstein greeted me from an upstairs window. It was a bizarre experience. Anna was completely unrecognisable. She was swathed in bandages, her eyes were puffy and bruised and there were stitches visible everywhere.

Later that night and despite our best efforts, our lovemaking came to nothing as we both agreed it was rather like having Tutankhamen messing around in your lady garden.

My birthday arrived. The kids had decided to make Anna and I breakfast in bed. We'd all agreed to spend the day on the beach, complete with a picnic also put together by their own fair hands. Nothing sums up the British summer better than a damp sandwich, a boiled egg and a squishy tomato with a side order of sand, now does it?

We were woken early by the kids, unsteady on their feet under the weight of three huge trays laden with an array of unusual breakfast options.

Everything had been arranged into patterns by three pairs of grubby little hands. There was a salami and lettuce face and albino toast covered in cold scrambled eggs sporting a grin made from olives. I was overwhelmed. They had gone to so much trouble. There was also a little pile of clumsily wrapped presents.

I turned to Anna with a huge smile that stretched from ear to ear. It was soon wiped off as Anna gave an irritated snort and rolled over, turning her back on proceedings.

I sat with my children and dutifully ate everything laid before me. The presents were an array of knick-knacks that had taken their fancy in the souvenir shops. Kids are like magpies at that age – unable to resist anything small and shiny.

Without warning, Anna suddenly jumped out of bed, distributing plates and debris before disappearing into the bathroom without so much as a 'happy birthday'. I thought perhaps she'd gone to retrieve her present, which she'd hidden in the airing cupboard. When I heard the sound of the shower being turned on, it was obvious I was wrong.

My children vanished downstairs to make the picnic. I desperately needed a drink, I felt so miserable. I couldn't understand what had happened to make Anna behave like this, especially on my birthday. I was also cross with myself that instead of being gratified by all the effort my three little people had made, I was upset because Anna was being a deliberate shithead. As I passed the bathroom, I knocked on the door and, through gritted teeth, thanked her for getting my special day off to such a good start.

Downstairs, I made myself a large cup of coffee, topped up with some cheap cherry brandy I'd found on offer at Lidls. Boy, that first hit of alcohol felt good.

I helped the kids make the sandwiches and pack everything away. As I was shelling boiled eggs, the front door banged loudly and from the front window, I spotted Anna scuttling off down the street.

It took another hour for me to get each of the kids dressed in appropriate beach gear, sort out their buckets and spades, then smear on globs of thick white sunscreen. Still no sign of Anna.

Sod it. I wasn't going to wait around for her to grace us with her presence. I would get on with the day as best I could, even if it meant being there more in body than mind.

As it was my birthday, I felt justified in making a stop on the way to the beach to buy a couple of bottles of champagne. I also hoped that Anna would turn up at some stage and we could put any bad feeling behind us with a shared glass of bubbly.

The kids loved every minute of being at the seaside. The eldest two painstakingly built sandcastles, which my youngest son then jumped on causing a near riot. The three of them discovered the joys of dune jumping and the thrill of racing away from the sea to avoid the breaking waves. As for me, I wallowed in self-pity, checking my mobile every five minutes for a text or call from Anna.

Lunchtime came and went. I ate very little, surreptitiously burying my over-Marmited sandwiches in the sand. I glugged my champagne direct from the bottle and must have looked like the epitome of inappropriate parenting to all the other beach-goers. A bottle in one hand and a cigarette in the other – more slummy mummy than yummy mummy.

Our day on the beach came to an end once I finished the second bottle. I was feeling desperate by this stage. I needed more booze. What the hell was Anna playing at?

It took an eternity to get back to the house as everyone in our little party was tired and dragging their feet. My heart sank even further when I realised Anna's car was no longer parked outside. I ran ahead, leaving the kids with the majority of our seaside trappings to carry.

It felt like walking into a ghost house. I knew she'd packed up without the need to check to see whether her stuff was still there. Upstairs in the bedroom, the bed remained unmade. Anna's bags had vanished.

A loud wail filled the house, echoing how I felt inside. It took me a few moments to realise I hadn't made the noise myself.

I ran downstairs half expecting to find one of my children had done some serious damage to themselves. I found my daughter standing in the space where Bugsy's cage had been, tears streaming down her face. All that was to be seen was the soiled sawdust Anna had kindly left for us to clear up.

Having comforted my daughter as best I could, I lit a cigarette and shaking like a leaf, sent Anna a text. "Fucking bitch, it's over."

CHAPTER 18

The rest of the week dragged by. I did my best for the sake of my children. I resisted the urge to up sticks and head back to Lincolnshire to beg Anna for mercy. Using every ounce of restraint I could muster, I didn't even send her any further texts or try calling her.

My resolve was down to a carefully monitored intake of alcohol. I'd discovered if I kept myself pleasantly inebriated but well below the point of complete intoxication, I could remain angry enough with Anna to avoid the urge to make contact.

I hadn't really thought through the practicalities of leaving her, especially since I'd only just set up my new business from her house. It didn't matter at this point in time. Despite feeling heartbroken, Anna had gone too far. How dare she abandon the kids and I whilst on her choice of holiday and in her bloody childhood county?

We went on seal-watching excursions, tried our hand at sea fishing (resulting in endless mackerel suppers) and spent hours playing bingo at the amusement arcade. Most days we ended up on the beach at some point. Given my head was completely up my arse most of the time, we all got sunburnt as I completely forgot about sunscreen after day one.

In a strange way, I found it quite a relief not having Anna around. At least our every move wasn't coupled with a running commentary. I could drink whatever I wanted, whenever I wanted, without having to resort to secretive methods of imbibing. And I didn't have to worry about what my children said or did with each passing moment.

I suppose the best way to put it is that we muddled through, me and my 'oh-so-tolerant' offspring. By the end of the week, I was almost sorry to be leaving. I hadn't a bloody clue about how I was going to make my business work and I wasn't looking forward to facing up to the reality of my current circumstances.

We paid one last visit to the pub in Wells, which we'd visited so often, we were almost regulars. As we walked in, the landlord asked me if it was the 'usual'. Indeed it was – three cokes, three bags of prawn cocktail crisps and two large G&Ts please.

By the time we left, I felt like Superwoman. Sod the Annas of this world, sod the Toms too, sod everyone. If I had been in a musical, I'd have burst into song and the kids would have joined in with some cute harmony from the back of the car.

Instead, I weaved my way back to Lincolnshire, well over the limit to drive. I took risks when over-taking, I stopped in lay-bys to pee in full view of passing traffic. I didn't give a toss. I was indomitable.

God knows how, but we made it back in one piece. I navigated my way to the place I'd rented for the summer. I went through the arse ache of unpacking all our stuff yet again. It was a good job I'd decided to take most of my clothes on holiday with me. At least I wasn't going to have to get in touch with Anna to ask for anything. Fat chance of that, anyway.

We still had plenty of food left over so the only immediate item on the agenda was a trip to the off-license. I could sense my alcohol levels dropping. The fact we were back in Anna Country was playing havoc with my emotions. Try as I might to convince myself otherwise, I was obsessed with the darned woman and she occupied my thoughts every waking moment.

As luck would have it, there was a pub directly opposite the cottage. It served good food and had a nice big play area for the kids.

For some reason, I rang MDH and brought him up to speed with my current set of circumstances. Without a moment's hesitation, he offered to drive up the coming weekend and I agreed. I was pining for some adult company and sensible conversation, even if it meant spending time with him.

Friday arrived and with it, MDH. We decided to go out for a meal *en famille* and found ourselves at a pub I'd not frequented before. They had a fantastic live band playing that night.

After eating, all five of us trooped out onto the dance floor. We seemed to be enjoying ourselves far too much for a family in the middle of a crisis. Of course, the fact that MDH and I had shared several bottles of good red wine helped.

We were the last to leave and when we got back to the cottage, we were too focussed on getting our sleeping children up to bed to notice a car parked opposite, its engine ticking over. As the night drew to a close neither were we aware our every move was being watched through binoculars.

***

It wasn't until the next morning, when I was woken by my phone ringing, that I became cognisant of the fact Anna had been stalking me over the last few days.

"Darling, I must see you," she pleaded with a tone to inspire pathos.

"Anna – no, it's over. I can't put up with the way you treat me or the kids any longer."

"I can change. I really can. I know it sounds daft but I get jealous of the kids. Please don't go back to MDH. I know he's staying with you."

"How on earth?"

"I'm parked over the road from your cottage."

Most people would have felt threatened on hearing this. But my heart started happily disco dancing. I did my best to maintain my cool.

"Anna, your behaviour isn't daft, it's not even childish. It's spiteful and selfish. You keep promising to change, to do things for the kids but nothing EVER changes. You always go back on everything you say. That's why we're living in this bloody Fisher Price doll's house for the summer. How do you expect me to trust you anymore?"

"Darling, no, don't finish with me, please, please..." her voice trailed off into sobs. It cut like a knife hearing her so upset.

"Please see me now?"

"I've only just woken up, go away."

"I've got all your post here. There's a lot of business mail. Please, darling?"

I went downstairs to peek out of the tiny little kitchen window. Sure enough, there she was in her car where she'd been camping out all night. My heart went out to her.

"Five minutes, that's all," I relented.

I let myself out of the cottage as quietly as I could. It was so early, even the children were still asleep. Anna looked dreadful – pale as a zombie with huge dark circles under her eyes. She was several pounds lighter than the last time I'd seen her. She grasped at my arm through the car window like some turn-of-the-century street beggar pleading with a well-off passer by. Although I found it all a bit disturbing, I ignored any doubts about her sanity I might have had.

"Let's go for a drive?" she suggested.

"Don't be daft, just let me have my post." I imagined Anna taking me hostage and never letting me see my children again.

"Please, baby, get in and let's have a talk. I am so sorry about everything."

I ached to get in the car and drive to her place, jump into bed and to kiss her tiny frame from head to toe. I was desperate to believe that she could change. I truly loved this pathetic creature. I mentally gave myself a good kicking and tried to behave like an adult.

"The kids will be awake soon. I'll call you." I gave her a watery smile and, taking the bundle of letters, I headed back to the cottage.

I could feel her eyes boring into the back of me. Don't look back. Don't look back. Looking back, I saw the same face staring at me as I had done the night we first met when we had to go through the exquisite pain of saying our goodbyes. Bloody woman.

CHAPTER 19

Moments after I closed the front door behind me, MDH appeared from upstairs. I felt like I was cheating on him all over again. Fortunately he'd not seen anything and remained in blissful ignorance.

We hired bikes and spent the day cycling. Oh what a surprise. Actually, there's a fantastic cycle path that circles Rutland Water – perfect for a family outing. So it made for a pleasant ride, just for once.

I made sure I'd taken a day's supply of alcohol with me, cleverly concealed in a couple of sports bottles attached to my bike. At one point I'd even considered filling a camelback with neat vodka so I could have booze on the move, but that seemed to be going too far even for me.

My phone vibrated with activity throughout the day. Anna sent a stream of texts declaring her undying love for me. I have to admit it gave me a nice, warm feeling. Who doesn't like to feel special? I also felt a bit of a fraud.

The only reason MDH had made best speed up to Lincolnshire was to help me through this split with Anna. He was probably secretly hoping we might get back together. He'd still not been able to find a job and was trying to set up a business himself without much success. No doubt I'd be useful to have around again.

I knew I'd never go back to him. Sitting next to MDH during a rest stop, I realised the smooth, soft contours of a woman appealed much more to me than a bulging masculine physique. As he stretched, he revealed a thicket of sweaty armpit hair and I almost gagged. I thought about Anna's gorgeous body that so entranced me. The image of her beautiful breasts flashed before me and I found myself instantly fantasising about her.

Throughout the weekend, MDH attempted to engineer circumstances to allow us to be on our own. It was so obvious he wanted to talk and try to begin some kind of a reconciliation. I didn't want to put him through rejection all over again so I swiftly un-engineered every opportunity he created.

Lying in bed that night, I could hold out no longer to my more primal desires. I responded to every one of Anna's texts. I had given in. Rather than wanting to turn back the clock and rebuild my old life, MDH's visit had only made me yearn for Anna more than ever. MDH was heading back to London after lunch on Sunday so I suggested to Anna that she came over later that evening once the kids were asleep. She agreed immediately and followed this up with a series of X-rated texts describing what she wanted to do to me in bed.

Another bike ride was planned first thing the following morning. Despite my decade-long aversion to cycling, I had to admit it felt good to be exercising again. I'd always loved going to the gym or running – anything I could do to keep the pounds at bay. My fat childhood had spawned an almost pathological fear of being overweight. Keeping it under control had proved to be a lifelong battle.

Since living with Anna it had been impossible to exercise. When HellFire had 'let me go', I'd suggested I'd get up early to go for a run before starting work. Anna poo-pooed this idea. She wanted to reclaim our mornings in bed together after the months of early starts. Although a member of the local gym herself, she rarely went. When I suggested joining, she'd dismissed it as being an unnecessary expense. I'd even tried sneaking out for a run on the days she worked away from home.

Somehow she'd found out and there had been hell to pay. So instead, I'd relied upon nervous energy and a diet of drink to keep my weight down.

My heart went out to MDH as he loaded up his car and gave the kids a big hug. I honestly wished things could have turned out differently – it would have been so much easier to live a 'normal life'. I wondered what it was in someone's genetic make-up that predisposed them to being gay? It certainly wasn't something I'd inherited from either of my parents.

I gave MDH a hug, making it as filial as possible, and the kids and I waved him off on his trip back to London.

Later on, I took the kids to the pub for a decent supper. I got myself in the mood for the evening ahead courtesy of a couple of large Baileys. Thanks to all the physical pursuits that weekend, the children went to bed without a murmur. I gave them all a bath and they fell asleep the moment their lovely little heads touched the pillow.

To ensure I looked as alluring as possible, I spent an hour or so getting ready and wore something that Anna had once said made me look sexy.

She knocked quietly on the door at the given time. When I opened it, there were tears in her eyes and we fell into each other's arms. God it felt good to have her so close to me again. I breathed in the smell of her hair, her perfume, her skin. After gulping down a couple of glasses of champagne, we headed straight upstairs.

The bedroom was filled with the flickering light of a dozen candles I'd lined up on the window-sill. That night proved to be the most intense and emotional sexual experience I'd ever have with Anna. It was the first and last time she actually felt present throughout. All the clichés you hear in love songs came true. It felt like we were the only two people who existed in the world. When I looked into her eyes, I caught an expression I'd never seen before. It was almost as if, for one night only, there was a flicker of her soul desperately trying to break free.

***

The rest of my summer with the kids flew by. Before you could say 'weak', I was moving back in with Anna who had kept to her promise to turn over a new leaf for the past fortnight.

However, her mask of change began to occasionally slip with the arrival of autumn. It started with the smallest of things. Irritation over the mess I created whilst making a cup of tea or for using the wrong knife to cut the bread.

One day, the weather was so glorious, I was sitting at 'her' desk whilst working in the conservatory as this allowed me a view of the garden. She'd been out on a sales call all morning, but the moment she got back she flew off the handle. Standing in the middle of the office, she ranted on about the fact I'd taken over the entire house and now had the cheek to lay claim to her desk. I moved back to mine immediately.

Then there was the time I was on the phone to a client arranging a photo shoot. We needed a couple of child models and to save money, I suggested roping in my lot. Anna, standing next to me, started furiously mouthing something unintelligible. I was still mid-conversation and despite this distraction, managed to complete the call with my reputation intact.

"What the hell was that all about?" I asked.

"Your bloody kids, they always get everything. Why not use my niece and nephew for the photo shoot? They're better looking anyway."

I was amazed. Yet more family members she rarely saw and here she was using them as some sort of stick to beat me with.

"Bitch!" I snapped.

1/ How dare she interfere?

And

2/ Have the gall to be so unpleasant about my children?

"Fat bitch!" she retorted.

She really knew how to hit where it hurt.

She also insisted on coming with me to my next new business meeting. Although I knew there was no real point, I agreed. I hoped that if she felt more involved in things, she might start behaving more like an adult. How wrong could I have been?

She began by disagreeing with everything I said in front of the potential client before switching off and staring around the room like a bored toddler. I half expected her to start picking her nose at any moment. It was horribly uncomfortable. I could see the disbelief in the eyes of everyone else. To this day I still don't know how I managed to get them to use my services following Anna's performance.

I continued to grow the business and was soon bringing in as much as I had earned at HellFire each month. Anna continued to talk about giving up her job to work with me full-time. Why she'd want to be part of a business she seemed to despise, I had no idea. She'd often laugh at the angles I came up with for press releases, dismissing them as silly nonsense. She refused to get on the phone to talk to people as she felt uncomfortable selling things. The only thing she wanted to do was create systems for the business. It was a ridiculous idea. The business was hardly of a size to warrant a box file, let alone 'systems'.

Weekends were the only times when Anna reverted to her alter ego. We'd go shopping in either Stamford or Oakham, have coffee, visit craft markets and you could guarantee we'd be glued to the TV every Saturday night.

I continued drinking on the sly. I was having to find ever more devious methods of hiding my stash now I was working from home. I'd rigged up a secret compartment in one of my desk drawers and had bottles located all over the house and garden. Whenever one of Anna's moods was imminent, I prepared myself with as much alcohol as I could sink without being obviously pissed.

Life settled into a pattern of uncertainty and I allowed a river of booze to help me go with the flow.

CHAPTER 20

Half-term was upon us and Anna did a U-turn on her decision to let the kids stay over. She was still holding a grudge about the photo shoot. So I spent it with them at my parents' again.

On returning to Lincolnshire, I found myself under constant scrutiny from dawn to dusk. Everything I did was criticised. Now that the business was doing well, she felt I should be paying rent for using the conservatory as an office, over and above my half of the mortgage.

This debate ended when I discovered Anna had arranged for all the household bills to be paid directly from the business account. She'd organised this whilst I'd been away with the kids without so much as a word. Furious, I pointed out this more than covered the extra money she'd been demanding for use of the office.

She also started having regular digs about my appearance. Sitting on the sofa one night she looked at my feet and told me I had the most enormous big toes she'd ever seen. Like something you'd see swinging around an ape house, she added. Although I laughed, my confidence took another knock. This was shortly followed by the loo seat breaking, the inference being that it was down to my hefty posterior.

Nothing was sacred. Her insults became increasingly personal and a little below the belt. I felt completely inadequate like some runt of the litter she'd taken in out of the goodness of her heart. My desire to take control of my body grew even stronger.

In the garage were a collection of very expensive mountain bikes Anna had bought when she was going through one of her many short-lived fads. I asked if I could borrow one so I could start cycling each day. She snorted and didn't even bother to explain why this wasn't going to happen. I knew if I tried to head out on one without her permission, she'd pull me off it or slash the tyres rather than let me have my way.

And then she did what she'd long been threatening. She gave up her job just like that, without warning, to take up her 'rightful role' as joint MD of my little PR business.

My drinking intensified. I seemed to spend more time drunk than sober although no one would have known most of the time. Functioning alcoholic – isn't that what they call someone?

On a sunny winter's Saturday, Anna and I were sitting outside on the decking enjoying a cup of tea and a cigarette. A weekend stretched ahead of us and I was enjoying a rare moment of contentment. Bugsy was out of his cage and scampering about performing acrobatics, much to the amusement of Anna who looked on dotingly.

"Let's go for a walk," I suggested. "It'll be lovely by Rutland Water today and it would make a nice change from going into town."

It was unusual for me to assume authority and suggest something. It was a mistake. The atmosphere changed immediately.

"Always thinking about exercise, aren't you? You're obsessed."

"A slight over-exaggeration on your part, I would suggest. Obsession is when someone starves themselves until they barely exist. What's that called? Oh, yes; anorexia."

She seemed startled that I'd had the temerity to respond in kind whilst completely sober.

"Sorry," I said, feeling immediately guilty for making a jibe at her expense. "We'll go to Stamford as planned," I added.

"You fucking bitch. I just want to be on my own today now. Do what you want. That probably means getting drunk."

She was absolutely right. She disappeared and from the exaggerated sounds coming from upstairs, I knew she was getting ready to go out by herself. I felt scared and abandoned.

I grabbed my handbag and exited the house. It felt childishly good to be the first one to leave, like I had scored a point over her. It was early and it seemed as though most of the village were still asleep. Knowing the day ahead of me was going to be a difficult one, I needed to get hold of some coping supplies.

I walked to the local shop. The two young girls, who were obviously Saturday staff, gave me an odd look as they scanned the six one-litre bottles of cider I was buying at nine a.m. in the morning. I also asked for three packets of Lambert & Butler Menthol. What a sad fucker I must have looked!

"Don't worry, it's not for me. It's for a party someone is having later. Much later."

Oh, shut up, you stupid cow, I told myself. They don't believe a word of it.

I headed to the field I'd discovered that first weekend I'd stayed at Anna's. It had since become a favourite hiding place of mine. I threw myself down in the middle, hidden from view by long-since-dead grass. The first drink of the day would soon have me feeling better, I reassured myself like some invisible parent. After quickly finishing an entire bottle, I was ready to do battle with Anna. Hiding the rest of my booty in the hedge, I made my way back to the house. But Anna had already gone out.

I let myself in and decided to punish myself further by going through all her drawers and cupboards in the hope of finding some of her hidden secrets. I wasn't disappointed. In the drawer under her side of the bed, pushed right to the back, was a carrier bag containing a bundle of love letters from Janie.

Reading them made me feel sick. They were peppered with phrases and words that replicated, verbatim, those Anna had written to me in the early days. There were photographs of the pair of them arm in arm – this cut like a knife given the fact I didn't have a single picture of the two of us together. There were cards, teddies and other love trinkets. Why would she keep all these, I wondered? Was Janie Anna's one true love? I knew that when Janie had left, Anna had taken an overdose and ended up in hospital for several days. If I was honest, I was a bit miffed she hadn't made an attempt on her life during our split the previous summer!

Having given myself a good emotional beating, I grabbed a bottle of brandy from the drinks cabinet. After a couple of mouthfuls, I stuffed it in my handbag and headed back to my field. I alternated between brandy and cider, well aware I was getting seriously drunk and it wasn't even midday.

After some further intense drinking, I felt the sudden need to chat to someone on the phone. I'd left my mobile on charge at the house. As I was going back to fetch it, I noticed that Anna's car was in the drive. Bollocks. I'd have to use the phone box in the middle of the village. If I rang my dad, I could reverse the charges.

Clinging on to my remaining bottles, I staggered up the hill to the phone. Naturally my father was distraught to hear his only daughter completely off her head. Instead of the consolatory words I was hoping for, he kept begging me not to have another drink. Now, as every child knows, if a parent insists on something, you'll do exactly the opposite, whether or not it's the right thing. As I was paying lip service to his pleas, I was knocking back the brandy.

All of a sudden, I felt giddy and realised I was on the point of collapse. I hastily said goodbye to him and fell backwards out of the phone box landing on the village green. Not so much a blackout this time as a drink-induced mini coma. It was hours before I came to and only then because I found myself being shaken roughly by a policeman. I seemed to be making a habit of this.

"Come on, I'll take you home," he said, levering me up from the ground.

I started to pick up the bottles, which had gone flying during my ignominious exit from the phone box. Officer Local wasn't having any of it and made me deposit them all in a nearby litter bin.

I was surprised to discover he knew where I lived. It transpired that someone had tipped off Anna as to my whereabouts and she had called the police. She let me in, apologised to the policeman and slammed the door behind me, pushing me into the sitting room where a fire was now blazing in the hearth.

"You drunken bitch, making a laughing stock of me in my village. How dare you behave like this in the place where I live!" she screamed.

"Your fucking fault. You treat me like shit. No wonder I drink."

Anna threw herself at me and I found myself sprawled on the ground for the second time that day. She sat on top of me, shouting as loudly as she could. I tried to push her off but she grabbed handfuls of my hair, twisting it to keep me pinned to the floor. Finding the strength from somewhere, I managed to get her off me and run upstairs.

She followed in close pursuit, grabbing at me again and again. I deliberately kicked out at one of her prize electric guitars to distract her. Anna wailed and then lunged at me. I felt her nails scratch my face. I was frightened. If I hadn't been so drunk, I would have been faster on my feet but I couldn't keep upright. Anna, on the other hand, was as sober as a judge and beat me at every turn. I was amazed at the ferocity of her attack. She was throwing punches, kicking me and spitting in my face.

I felt myself fall backwards down the stairs. Unhurt, I made a dash for the sitting room where I spotted a toy gorilla perched on the sofa – another love gift from yet another ex-lover. It sang a ridiculous song when you pressed a button and waved its arms in time. I'd always hated it.

I grabbed it and was about to throw it at Anna. Worried it might really hurt her, I lobbed it onto the fire instead. Flames began licking around it and the gorilla suddenly sprang into action. It managed one last pitiful refrain of "Feeling Hot, Hot, Hot" before making its way to the great toyshop in the sky.

The absurdity of the situation brought a smile to my face and I looked over at Anna, hoping she would see the funny side too. She had something in her hands and I realised it was a solid glass ashtray, which she hurled at me with sheer hatred.

I was shaking uncrontrollably. Anna was coming for me again, her arms outstretched like something from the *Thriller* video. I lost any desire to carry on brawling. I didn't want to fight like this. I made for the back door and disappeared into the garden. She didn't follow me this time. I heard the sound of bolts being drawn on the back door. She had locked me out.

I found one of my special hiding places and uncovering a bottle filled with a mixture of spirits, gulped it down to calm my nerves. As I reappeared from behind the garden shed, I saw Anna staring stony-faced at me through the conservatory window. I was reminded once again of the night we'd first met and how pitiful she'd looked when we parted. How different she looked now.

I walked over and tried to reason with her through the glass. I pleaded, I cried, I told her how much I loved her. She remained unmoved and started mocking me as the tears rolled down my cheeks.

Out of the corner of my eye, I spotted the coal bucket sitting by the back door. I grabbed it and swung it at the kitchen window, which disintegrated into a thousand tiny shards. I pulled at the jagged glass still in the frame with my bare hands. Reaching inside, I opened the window and started to climb through. Anna appeared, talking on the phone.

"Yes, she's just broken the window and is now climbing in. I'm scared."

"Anna please, can we talk?"

"Thank you. Don't be long."

"Who are you talking to?"

"The police… again."

"No, Anna. Tell them it's OK. We'll be fine, we just need to talk. Please, Anna?"

But she wasn't listening. She just walked out of the room, calm and composed. I caught sight of myself in a mirror. I had scratches down my face, my clothes were filthy from my various adventures of the day and my eyes were bloodshot. I hardly looked like the innocent party in all this. Then there was the evidence – Alice Bellamy, in the kitchen with the coal bucket.

When the police arrived, I had imagined we'd all sit down around the table together and have a cosy little chat about the dangers of drinking. I'd get my wrists slapped before a line was drawn under the sorry affair.

The police car arrived complete with a blue flashing light. They had a brief word with Anna before coming in to arrest me. It was as simple as that. I was put in cuffs and escorted to the police car. This couldn't be happening. My head was pushed down as I got into the car just like you see them do on the telly and off we went.

Our destination was Melton Mowbray Police Station. Before being banged up with the assorted drunks and renegades, I was made to endure further humiliation. Everything was emptied out of my handbag, the contents duly recorded and bagged up. My shoelaces were removed from my trainers and my jewellery taken away. Apparently this was standard procedure to ensure I didn't have anything about my person that could be used in a suicide attempt. Lord knows how much damage you could inflict on yourself with a pair of Miss Selfridge clip-on earrings, but there you go. I was being processed like a criminal and it felt sordid, grubby and degrading.

I tried having a laugh with the coppers but it fell completely flat. I asked whether I could keep the picture of my kids I carried with me everywhere, but I was even refused that privilege.

As tradition has it, I was allowed to make one phone call. I was tempted to call Anna. I was desperate to hear her voice reassuring me it had all been a dreadful mistake and that she was in her car and on her way to fetch me. Instead I rang MDH and asked him to let my parents know about the latest scrape I had got myself into. I was pleased he didn't give me a lecture.

After that, I was confined to a single cell - a plain concrete room with a ledge for a bed and a toilet without a seat. No doubt a toilet seat presented another potential suicide hazard. The window even had bars on it. What a cliché I had become. How had my life come to this? I was a middle-aged woman with three children and a respectable business and here I was, locked away in a town best known for its pork pies. What a complete load of crap.

An eternity went by before some butch policewoman threw a couple of blankets at me and I was left alone again. To add insult to injury, my period started. Despite banging relentlessly on the door, I was ignored and had to create a makeshift sanitary pad out of scratchy Izal toilet paper.

It was impossible to sleep because of all the noise. Drunks were being incarcerated throughout the night, wailing and postulating loudly. The effects of yesterday's binge were wearing off and I was experiencing one of the worst hangovers I'd ever had.

Time ticked away interminably. I was freezing and the blankets that had been supplied had the density of cobwebs. My whole body ached and, for the first time, I noticed the cuts on my hands where I had tried to climb through the window to get to Anna.

Even though she had been instrumental in putting me here, my main concern was whether Anna would have me back. I found myself rocking backwards and forwards in tears. Not for this lesson in ultimate degradation but at the prospect of losing Anna for good.

As a dirty streak of daylight began to show itself through the barred window, I heard the cell door open. I looked up to see an older PC standing there.

"All right love, fancy a cup of tea?"

"Oh, yes, please, and I don't suppose there's a chance of a cigarette, is there?"

"I'll see what I can do." And, with a gentle smile, he shut the door on me.

As good as his word, he came back and I was led into a small courtyard with a high wall topped by razor wire. My head was spinning and I felt so incredibly sick, I had to sit down to drink my tea. He'd managed to rustle up a cigarette, which he lit for me. Shakily taking a drag, I asked what would happen next.

"You'll have to wait for the duty solicitor to arrive so you can make your statement then you'll probably be allowed to go, pending prosecution."

"Prosecution? I haven't done anything wrong!"

He grinned.

"Funny isn't it, no-one in here has ever done anything wrong. Domestic, was it?"

"I suppose you'd call it that. So, when you say prosecuted, what's that likely to mean?"

"No idea, my love. Right, time to go back inside, I'm afraid".

The sounds of everyday life just beginning in the real world were abruptly snuffed out as the large iron door banged behind me and I was returned to my cell.

A further torturous two hours passed before the duty solicitor arrived. She turned out to be a bright woman roughly the same age as me. She carefully explained that I would need to give a statement, which would be recorded on tape. She would be present throughout together with two policemen. It was looking unlikely that charges would be pressed as the police hadn't been able to get hold of Anna. In all likelihood, the case would be dropped. Nevertheless, I still had to be 'processed'.

Everything happened swiftly after that. I gave my statement as prepped by my solicitor. I was then taken to a room where I had my photo taken – one of those where you hold a number, stand face on and then turn for your profile pic. Not one for the family album. My fingers were covered in black ink by a chatty little policeman. He rattled on as if we were doing potato printing at nursery school rather than taking my fingerprints.

I was then informed I was free to go and that my Uncle George was waiting outside to pick me up.

Uncle George? MDH must have rung my mother who, in turn, got hold of her younger brother. I'd forgotten he'd moved to Lincolnshire years ago. Oh God, how embarrassing! He had four children who were all shining examples of upstanding citizens.

I collected all my belongings and decanted them from their official police bags. Heading outside, the sunlight seemed dazzling after my troglodyte night in the clink.

"Alice."

I heard my uncle's voice boom across the car park. He was standing with his arms outstretched and a big smile on his face. He looked like a giant teddy bear.

"George, I am so, so sorry. What awful circumstances for a family reunion! Thanks for coming to fetch me."

"That's what family is all about, isn't it?"

When I got into his car, he didn't berate me or offer any pearls of wisdom, he simply suggested that I should stay with him and my Aunty Tina for the time being. The plan was to drive over to Anna's and collect enough of my things to see me through a couple of weeks. That would give me the space to decide what to do next.

My stomach was churning as we retraced my journey of last night in reverse. I wondered whether Anna would be at home. She had made certain I hadn't taken my keys with me so we might not be able to get in. Hiding my things was something she did quite regularly when we argued. Be it my phone, my laptop or my keys. Another way to control me, I suppose.

As we pulled into the drive, Anna's car was parked exactly where it had been yesterday. The bedroom curtains were still drawn. George told me to stay in the car whilst he spoke to her. After knocking on the door several times, she appeared in the bedroom window looking ghastly.

"I'm Alice's uncle. I just want to collect some of her things so she can come and stay with us!" he shouted up at her.

"No, I don't want you in my house."

"Well, then, I'll come in with Alice while she packs some things."

"No."

And with that, she vanished inside, putting me in mind of the White Rabbit hastily scurrying way.

George got back in the car.

"Never trust a woman who paints her face like a clown," he said to me.

My God, he was so right. For some reason, her tattooed features bore an uncanny resemblance to Jack Nicholson as The Joker that day. I still loved her and felt guilty for even thinking that, let alone having a chuckle at her expense.

Our mirth was interrupted when a car pulled up behind us. It was the village doctor, Roger. Anna had quite a history with him. He'd been the one to discover her when she'd taken her overdose following Janie's departure.

George got out of the car and went to shake hands with him. I watched the two of them in the rear-view mirror as they had an affable exchange. Roger then knocked on the front door and this time, Anna opened it and let him in. George got back into the car and explained to me that Roger was going to have a chat with her and try to persuade her to let me get my things.

Twenty minutes later, Roger reappeared and beckoned to both of us. As we walked inside, I could see Anna's eyes were puffy from crying. The four of us sat down around the dining room table.

"Anna doesn't want you to leave," Roger explained. "I've told her that it's not really the done thing to keep involving the police in your affairs and it's not doing either of your reputations in the village much good."

"I'm taking my niece back with me," George insisted.

"Please let me talk to Alice alone?" Anna pleaded.

Tears filled her eyes again and she gave me a baleful look.

I nodded. Both men reluctantly left the room.

"Darling, please don't leave, we can make this work. Things got out of hand, that's all."

I stared down into my lap knowing I didn't have the strength of character to go back to my uncle's. I wanted to stay with Anna and to feel loved again. I didn't say anything. She came and sat next to me and took my hands in hers, gently caressing my injuries.

"Please sweetheart, everyone goes through bad times," she said, gently lifting my chin with her hand.

Not everyone ends up spending the night in the cells though, I thought. Instead of saying this, I heard myself saying, "I love you Anna. Of course I'll stay."

Although my uncle didn't think it was the best decision, he didn't reprimand me but simply reiterated that I could call him any time. Having shaken hands with Roger again, he headed off. Roger gave us both a hug, begged us to take good care of each other then disappeared too.

Anna bathed my hands, made me a large mug of sweet tea and a plate piled high with buttered toast. It was bitter sweet. After my dark night of the soul, it was all I had yearned for and yet I felt like I was being a traitor to myself. Any time there was drama in our relationship, or Anna felt that she was losing me, she changed back to the woman I had first fallen in love with.

We slept for the rest of the day – a restless, uncomfortable sleep. I still felt shoddy after the whole experience despite having taken several showers.

For the first time, I couldn't get rid of the feeling I had violated something deep within me. Perhaps I'd actually muddied my soul this time?

Part of me regretted not having gone with my uncle. As I looked at Anna whilst she slept, I experienced a moment of loathing I'd never felt towards her before. Love and hate. They do say there's a fine dividing line between them. Lying there, I realised just how fine. It made me feel a new kind of sadness.

CHAPTER 21

I lay in bed the next morning going over and over the events of the past few days. Something inside was telling me it was the time to face the fact my drinking was a little out of control, to say the least.

Anna was still asleep. When she finally did come to, she rolled across to my side of the bed, purring and making romantic overtures. Sex was the last thing on my mind.

Having taken her tea in bed, I headed for the office and googled alcoholism. Thousands of sites instantly appeared on my screen. Alcoholics Anonymous kept popping up but I didn't consider this an option. AA was for sad sods in dirty overcoats who drank out of bottles secreted within brown paper bags. I certainly didn't belong in this category.

I had no idea what I was looking for. Thoughts of The Priory flashed through my mind but I wasn't really an addict or in a salary bracket that could afford such a luxury.

Suddenly one site leapt out at me. It stated, simply enough, that affordable treatment was available throughout the UK. I dialled the number and my call was answered immediately. Having briefly described my situation, I was told to expect a call back within the hour.

Sure enough, a woman called Kim rang me fifteen minutes later. She managed a treatment centre just outside Lincoln and told me if I was serious about getting help, she would do an assessment over the phone. Definitely. After answering a few questions, Kim told me I'd benefit from a stay at the centre sooner rather than later. I booked myself in the very next day.

When I told Anna she nodded slowly, seemingly lost in thought. Eventually she came over and gave me a half-hearted hug. Although I'd been shit scared about losing Anna throughout all of my drunken antics, something inside me had changed. I'd reached a point where my only option was to go into treatment and I realised I was doing this for myself. Not to please Anna. It was a good job really as she didn't seem as delighted about the idea as I'd imagined.

I was surprised.

***

I set off early the next day having not touched a drop of drink for over twenty-four hours.

After winding through increasingly narrow lanes, I turned up a long drive and finally came to a stop in front of a building straight from the set of a Hammer Horror film. Standing on the front doorstep were a group of white-faced, chain-smoking zombies – the inmates. Bloody hell, I certainly didn't belong here. I was tempted to turn the car around and make a rapid exit to the nearest pub. But I had promised myself that I would go through with this. There was no turning back.

The ghostly apparitions had vanished by the time I'd parked and got my bag out of the car. As I walked inside, an amazing sense of peace came over me like I had just been given a giant invisible hug.

A jolly chap called Graeme bounced up to greet me and wrapped his arms around me. He wanted to ask me a few more questions about my drinking and told me to answer with complete honesty. I followed him into a cosy sitting room.

"Well, what do you think?" I asked him once we'd finished going through his assessment.

"About what?"

"Am I an alcoholic?"

"Absolutely. No shadow of a doubt. It's whether you believe you are."

Without hesitation, I smiled at him and nodded.

"Yes, I am."

The relief was palpable. I started shaking and tears streamed down my face although I didn't even realise I was crying until Graeme pushed a box of tissues in my direction. It felt incredible to give in to the truth at last. How bizarre I'd been in denial only minutes beforehand.

Graeme then gave me a tour of the place. Lime House turned out to be very different inside from its gaunt Gothic exterior. The only thing that bothered me was discovering that I was to share a bedroom. I pointed out that I'd prefer a room to myself as it would make it easier for me to focus on my treatment. Graeme smiled and nodded, saying he'd see what he could do.

Rehab wasn't going to be a holiday that was for sure. Everyone had to be up by seven a.m. and have finished breakfast by nine a.m. in time for the first session of the day. Clients – not inmates, as Graeme corrected me – attended two group sessions before lunch. In the afternoon there were assignments to complete as well as one-to-one counselling before the group got back together for the final session of the day. After supper, people continued their studies or attended a local AA meeting.

I baulked at this. I wasn't a street drunk and AA was all about God, wasn't it? I didn't want to do the God thing. Graeme just smiled and nodded at me again.

Clients were also expected to clear up after themselves following each meal, which included loading the dishwasher. They also had to do their own washing and keep all the shared rooms clean and tidy. It wasn't about cheap labour. The point was to encourage people to start taking responsibility for themselves and others again, Graeme explained.

The atmosphere at Lime House was magical. It reminded me of the feeling I used to get on Christmas Day when I was a child. Everyone seemed so calm and relaxed. I wanted to be like that. To feel comfortable within myself, without the need for alcohol.

Most of the clients stayed for a minimum of a month but that was out of the question for me. I couldn't afford the time or the money. All I could commit to was a week. I prayed the penny would drop in the following seven days.

I was introduced to everyone else in the group. Whether you had been there for two weeks or two hours, there was only one group. I was surprised to find there were as many women as men and that most of them were fairly senior business types. I was annoyed with myself for calling everyone zombies earlier.

The majority of them had stayed initially at the detox unit some miles away in Barnsley before transferring to Lime House. As well as needing to be medically assisted in the process of coming off the booze, alcoholics have to be monitored by specialist staff, as it can be a dangerous process. I thanked my lucky stars that I'd found the place when I did. Had I left my decision a week or so longer, I would have had to go through detox too, Graeme later informed me.

Another thing about going into recovery is that you become versed in a completely new lingo. "Rock bottom", for example, is the point an alcoholic reaches when they feel desperate about life because they can't live with or without drink. It's at that point they're ready to do something about it. Only then can treatment work.

So if a well-meaning friend or family member tries to make someone get help, was it doomed, I asked? More than likely. I now wanted this so badly - I was sick and tired of being sick and tired. Another favourite phrase of recovering alcoholics.

That night we ate supper sitting around a couple of communal tables – there were eighteen of us in total. We helped ourselves to comfort food of the highest order – stodgy macaroni cheese with coleslaw and great hunks of bread and butter. There was steamed jam sponge and custard for pudding.

Whilst we were eating everyone chatted openly about their issues. Quite a few of my peers had dual addictions including the youngest in our group, a lovely bubbly girl of eighteen. She disappeared straight after supper and I was told she'd gone to make herself sick as she was both an alcoholic and a bulimic.

After dinner I found myself on the front doorstep having a cigarette with everyone else, having done our chores. I had joined the ranks of the 'living dead'.

When I got upstairs to my room, I discovered I was stuck with sharing. My room mate, Niamh, a delightful Irish woman I'd briefly met earlier in the day, was getting ready for bed. We clicked instantly and it was like being in a dorm at boarding school. She tried to explain a little more about rehab, but I became increasingly confused. I think I had expected some kind of magic toolbox to use every time I was tempted to drink. I settled down to sleep having no idea what to expect over the coming week.

There were owls hooting outside but, other than that, the house was perfectly still. I realised I was hangover free for the first time in ages and I loved it. I'd also completely forgotten to ring Anna. Oh what the hell.

I was too exhausted to call now. It was one of the best nights' sleep I'd had for a very long time.

***

After breakfast the next morning, I got chatting to some of the others whilst helping to load the dishwasher. Once again I was struck by everyone's honesty about how bad their drinking had become and the awful things they had got up to. It was a huge relief to realise that I was not the lone oddball I'd assumed I was. As an alcoholic, you become isolated by your drinking, inhabiting a solo world of secrecy and lies. In the end, the only thing that motivates you is working out how you're going to get your next drink.

Graeme was leading the first session of the day. We lay on the floor whilst he read some platitudes from a book. I looked around to see if I could find a co-conspirator to have giggle with, as it seemed a little inane to me. I found I was on my own – the rest of the group were deep in thought. I felt like an idiot for the second time in as many days.

Following our meditation, it was time for someone to talk us through their Step One of the twelve-step programme. Aha – finally the answer I'd been looking for. Initially, the Steps seemed like gobbledygook to me, written in some Middle Earth language that would have sat well on a slate carved by elves.

The Twelve Steps

You soon discover that giving up drinking is the easy bit. What's hard is living your life and facing up to reality without using drink as a crutch.

The Twelve Steps are there to help you learn how to do this. At the risk of sounding like a trite self-help book, they are the path to spiritual enlightenment.

Once you get your head around them, you can pretty much find the answer to anything bothering you. I've often heard it said that anyone, alcoholic or not, would benefit from the Twelve-Step programme and it's probably very true.

I assumed, given I only had a week at Lime House, they would fasttrack me so I could complete all of the Steps whilst I was there. I said as much to Kim who gave me a wry smile, which in hindsight was the polite equivalent of "bollocks to that as an idea".

We kept being told that we had to work the Steps if we wanted them to work for us. What did that mean, for goodness sake? It sounded like something from a Jane Fonda fitness video. The God word also cropped up rather too often for my liking. Did this mean that unless I had some 'road to Damascus' experience whilst I was there, I would never be free from the demon drink?

Someone explained to me that I could substitute the word God for Higher Power, which still sounded pretty bloody religious to me. But apparently a higher power could be anything you are prepared to put your faith in other than yourself. It could be a chair, my group at Lime House or even a bar of chocolate. Now you're talking, I thought.

Strangely, I started to get my head around the idea of a higher power – it was like having an invisible friend you could talk to about anything without being judged. A mute Jiminy Cricket!

Step One involved revealing just about every terrible thing you'd done when drunk. Before 'going public', you had to write down answers to a series of questions on a work sheet. To do it thoroughly often took a couple of days.

Once finished, it provided the basis of your 'confession', which had to be made in front of the entire group. After listening to a number of Step Ones, I was humbled by the strength everyone showed in revealing their deepest and darkest secrets.

As if that wasn't bad enough, the therapists would then weigh in with questions and statements that really had you squirming. By the end of the morning, the Step One candidate was emotionally bereft, exhausted and unable to stop crying – the rest of us didn't feel that great either. My Step One was scheduled for Wednesday, so I had a huge task ahead of me to pull together all the sordid details of my drunken past.

CHAPTER 22

Eating dinner that night, I was struck by the fact that the group shared a very similar sense of humour. It was a truly morbid black humour. I felt a real connection with all these shattered human beings and, given everything we were going through, it was bizarre how much time we spent laughing.

Before I could become too sentimental, I was brought back to reality when I heard my name being called out. I was to be bussed off to an AA meeting along with four others from the group.

"Do I have a choice?" I asked the genial Australian therapist who was organising the trip.

"Yes, you can choose to remain an alcoholic if you prefer," he grinned and left the dining room.

At that point I decided to give myself up unquestioningly to the whole process and leave my assumptions about AA in the past. I realised that I had been more of an observer of the rehab process until that point, almost arrogantly considering myself above it all. What a stupid cow.

On arriving at the meeting, I thought we'd come to the wrong place and accidentally turned up at some parish council do. Everyone looked so respectable and far too posh for AA. The same warmth I had felt at Lime House pervaded the small room we were all squeezed into. We were made to feel welcome and each of us was handed a cup of tea. I was also delighted to find endless plates piled high with homemade cakes and an amazing variety of biscuits.

The meeting was 'opened' by a chap who talked for a while about his own personal experience of alcoholism before inviting people to contribute to the dialogue. I remember feeling intensely embarrassed by the lengthy silences that punctuated the meeting. They made me feel so uncomfortable I felt like getting up and doing a song and dance routine to fill them. Eventually I learnt to accept them just like everyone else did. They were as much a part of the meeting as the talking bits, I discovered.

A middle-aged woman who looked like my first headmistress began to speak. As her story unfolded, I realised I was hanging on to her every word and felt completely in awe of her. Her adventures had included crashing her car into the neighbour's hedge, wetting the bed at night after binge drinking plus countless blackouts when she'd no idea what, or whom, she'd got up to. Ultimately, her behaviour had led to the departure of her husband and her grown-up children had disowned her.

Since coming to AA, she had been sober for seven years and now had her family back as well as being completely content with her life. Oh, the very thought of being satisfied with your lot was enough to enthral me. When the meeting ended, I went across to her and thanked her for sharing her story – she gave me a huge hug. The penny had dropped. From that moment I knew I was committed to staying sober. I was filled with such an excitement about the future it felt like every cell in my body was cheering.

As well as focussing as hard as I could during all the sessions the next day, I threw myself into my Step One. It was harrowing to dredge up all the old memories and remember some of the things I had done. It made me wince. At the end of the day, I stayed behind in the group therapy room so I could work on my Step One before dinner. There was a quiet knock on the door and Anna walked in.

"Hello sweetie, I thought you might like a visit?"

I didn't know what to say. Although I was touched that she'd driven all this way to see me, I felt irritated that she hadn't run the idea past me first. To be honest, all I wanted to think about was my treatment and Anna was not the best person to have around if it was peace of mind you were after.

"Darling, how lovely to see you. I've missed you," I lied.

"I've spoken to Graeme and it's fine for us to pop out for something to eat, as long as you don't, you know, drink".

"Oh. Well, of course, I won't drink, but..."

I wanted to say that I'd prefer to stay put and eat with everyone else that evening. However, I knew she'd have a strop and that wouldn't be particularly productive for me at that moment in time. Instead, I dutifully got my coat, made my excuses and let Anna drive us to the nearby town for an Indian meal.

Although I had only been at Lime House for a couple of days, it felt very strange to be out in the real world. I didn't feel ready. In the end, we ate very little and returned to the treatment centre having only been gone for about an hour. It was such a relief to get back. I'd imagined Anna would push off immediately but she came in and sat with everyone for the rest of the evening. I resented her presence. This was my special place.

"I'll see you again on Saturday," she reminded me as she left, making a big display of kissing me. Saturday was family day – my parents were due to turn up as well so we could all sit with a therapist and talk about my issues. Oh joy.

When we got outside, she took me in her arms and held me tightly.

"Now, don't go falling for any of those other alcoholics, will you?" she said, only half-jokingly, as she got into her car.

I watched her car disappear and I felt pity for her. Something inside me was changing and that included my feelings for Anna. I knew I still loved her, but I wasn't certain that was going to be enough moving forward. I dismissed these thoughts and went up to my room to finally finish my Step One.

***

I felt nervous as hell as I took my place in the centre of the room. My Step One remains a bit of a blur to this day but a defining moment has stayed with me with pin sharp clarity. I was describing my recent binge that had led to my arrest and ultimately to Lime House.

"I must have looked like the village drunk," I said as a throwaway line to the group.

"And why would that be?" Graeme asked.

I sat there open-mouthed and shocked before whispering, "Because I was the village drunk."

"We can't hear you," Graeme said.

"Because I was, I *am*, the village drunk," I said clearly.

Well, bugger me. The revelation sent me reeling. How could I face anyone in that village again? Would I have to go around making amends to everyone? Perhaps I could get a T-shirt that read – IT'S OK, I DON'T DRINK NOW.

My face felt as if it was burning up. Niamh told me I went the colour of beetroot. For the second time tears were popping out of my eyes like some cartoon character and I hadn't a clue I was crying. Well, if I was looking for a second epiphany, then there it was.

More and more confessions spilt out of me like an overflowing barrel. No one batted an eyelid or looked disgusted. Everyone had been there, done that, during their lives as alcoholics. This included drunk driving with our children in the car, lying and cheating, sneakily hiding bottles around the house and stealing. The energy and effort that we all put into our drinking was amazing.

STEALING

One of the things I did a lot when I was pissed was steal things. Aged fifteen and high as a kite on Cherry B, I'd managed to do my entire Christmas shopping (well, nicking) in a couple of hours. Everybody was taken aback at the quality of their gifts that year – hand-stitched leather purses, an Oriental chess set and even a large, decorative mirror. How on earth had I managed to afford these, I was asked? I shrugged – sold a few things at school and saved hard.

Thankfully, my thieving became a little more benign in later life.

Balloons were my favourite hoard. Not just one or two, but as many as I could get my hands on at whatever posh do I was attending. After one ball I'd been to, I'd helped myself to the balloons from every table. As per normal, MDH had not come with me at the last minute for some reason, so I had taken the opportunity to get paralytic in the company of a gay male friend.

I knew I was too drunk to drive home so I decided to stuff all the balloons into the people mover, which was parked in some London backstreet. Early the next morning, MDH woke me up demanding to know where the car was. And I couldn't tell him. I had no idea where I'd left it. He duly headed off on his bike to comb the streets in the vicinity of Kensington in search of it. Of course, when he found it, he first had to dispose of all the balloons in order to fit his bike inside for the drive home.

It gave me immense pleasure to think of his Lycra-clad figure popping sixty helium-filled balloons in the cold light of day.

After an hour-and-a-half of confession plus the input of Graeme and his laser-precise comments, I felt exhausted. It was like being that giant bronze god Talos in the film *Jason and the Argonauts* – the one whose valve was removed from his heel resulting in all his power and strength ebbing away. I felt just like an empty vessel, stripped of everything.

All the excuses I had created to justify being an alcoholic swirled around in my head like dead leaves. And then they vanished. Mantras I had clung to since my teenage years such as "I had an unhappy childhood", "my parents both drank too much", "my mother preferred her foster child to me" scurried away pathetically.

All of them were true, but so what? Deal with it. You're an adult now.

It was time to accept that most people have issues to contend with. Not everyone uses them as excuses for not participating fully in life.

Another eye-opener was the discovery I'd almost certainly been an alcoholic since my mid teens. Apparently, the moment you start drinking alcoholically is the moment you stop developing emotionally. Jeez – I had been a petulant adolescent for over twenty-five years. No wonder my parenting skills weren't 'all that'. I had a lot of maturing to do over the next few years. I started wondering what I wanted to be when I grew up? Sober would be a good start.

CHAPTER 23

The end of the week arrived. Tomorrow my nearest and dearest would be arriving to pick over my desiccated carcass like crows. I didn't expect to achieve much personally, but I knew it was an important part of the healing process for my family. Recovery wasn't just about me!

My mum was in denial and didn't think I had a problem. My dad would be emotional and say nothing that could be construed as a criticism of me. Despite all my failings, he still thought the sun shone out of my gluteus maximus.

And Anna – what role would she play, I wondered? My bet was on the concerned and loving martyr who had suffered extensively at my hands. I was certain she would try and talk about some particularly unsavoury moments from my recent past in a bid to shock my parents.

She would have loved nothing better than for them to disown me so she could have me all to herself. Unfortunately for her, they were as attached to me as Velcro to a female wrestler's armpit. And I had been a bit of an armpit, let's face it.

I took myself off on a long walk to find the village church. I wouldn't have felt comfortable being on my own in the middle of nowhere in the past. I had always been paranoid about being attacked or abducted, but many of the fears I'd clung on to had simply buggered off over the last few days.

I sat on a hard wooden pew and savoured the tranquillity of my surroundings. I found myself praying – well, chatting – to someone. It wasn't God as such but simply a force for good. My Higher Power, I suppose. It was comforting to hold forth about the things that were bothering me.

That evening, I volunteered to go to another AA meeting. I found tremendous strength from being with a group of recovering drunks. The endless choice of homemade cakes and biscuits were also another rather good reason to attend.

Saturday morning came around and with it, Anna. As I watched her walk down the corridor, I was aware how attractive I still found her. I wondered if lust was the basis of my entire relationship with her? Had I also found the endless rounds of fighting and making up stimulating? Had I mistaken danger for love?

She seemed a little cooler than she had earlier in the week. It turned out she was irritated that she'd had to manage the business on her own for a week. She would have continued moaning had my parents not arrived.

My father gave me a hug and the sort of look normally reserved for some mutt at an RSPCA rehoming centre. My mother asked for a glass of wine instead of the coffee she'd been offered. Not the smartest move, Mater.

I knew my parents didn't care in the slightest for Anna. They felt there was something not quite right about her. She was a 'cold fish', as my mother had described her. It was strange watching Anna with other people. Chameleon-like, she seemed to assume the identity of those around her. It had only just struck me that there was no real continuity to her personality.

Today, all of her sentences seemed to begin with the phrase "Oh my goodness," and everything about her seemed stilted. When Niamh briefly joined us and filled the room with her particular high-voltage Irish energy, it spotlighted Anna's lack of individuality.

The allotted hour for our family session presented itself. I was asked to talk first. I handed out cards that I'd written the previous night to all three of them. They contained heartfelt apologies for all the hurt I had caused. I then went on to describe my experience at Lime House and my commitment to staying sober.

I had imagined it was going to be a lot more intense than it turned out to be. My father used the session for one of his comedy routines whilst my mother kept repeating she didn't believe I was an alcoholic. After all, she had been 'an exemplary mother'.

As I'd expected, Anna reminded everyone of my recent criminal activities and subsequent arrest. As she delivered the news, she cast a triumphant look at my parents hoping for some kind of shock-horror reaction. However, given the fact they were well aware of my night in the clink, neither of them batted an eyelid.

The session came to an end.

I was pleased that my parents went away feeling positive about my progress and more importantly, better about themselves. Actually, I was just pleased that everyone went away.

There was no such thing as a weekend off for the Lime House clientele. I returned to my group in the afternoon to continue working on the Steps. As I settled into my seat, it struck me I only had two more nights left there. The thought terrified me. Would I be able to stay sober in the big wide world? It was so comfortable being at Lime House that I hadn't given any thought to sobriety beyond its four walls.

I cornered Graeme later and asked him how best to deal with real life. Get yourself a sponsor and find your local AA meetings – simple as that. I got straight onto it using a book that listed every AA meeting in the world. It was gobsmacking that you could find one in almost every town or city across the globe.

Within two hours, I'd sorted myself out with a sponsor. I'd managed to speak to her on the phone and she'd agreed to meet up with me the following Tuesday and take me to a meeting close to Stamford. I felt better and more confident about not drinking, no matter what happened when I left Lime House.

On Sunday, the therapy team spent a lot of time with me mapping out the Step work I'd need to complete by myself or with my sponsor. My address book was filled with the names and contact details of everyone in my group – all truly sincere about wanting to stay in touch. It was sad to learn years later that most of them subsequently went back to drinking, three of them died due to drink-related illness and, of the eighteen, only two of us remain sober to this day.

Niamh and I chatted and giggled for an hour or so once we'd gone to bed. Like me, she was concerned about her future. Her husband was a heavy drinker and she knew if she stopped accompanying him on drunken forays to the local pub, he'd find some other woman to share his bottle and his bed.

I voiced my hopes that Anna would feel more secure now I'd stopped drinking and that things would settle into a more comfortable routine. We both nodded half-heartedly, neither of us really convinced that either of our partners were capable of change.

When I woke the next day, there was still an hour before breakfast. I packed my things and read through everything I'd learnt that week. I was determined to be a grade A student of sobriety.

Lime House had a traditional way of saying goodbye to people when they left. It was rather like someone leaving the Big Brother house. Everyone lined up either side of the hallway and the 'graduate' walked down the middle. You were cheered and clapped and hugged

211

from either side as you made your way outside. Niamh was the last person to say goodbye and she handed me a card and a small plant. I could feel the tears welling up as we held each other tightly before I got into my car and started the engine.

Suddenly I felt lost and lonely again. In days of yore, this would have been the perfect excuse to find the nearest pub and knock back a couple of drinks to steady my nerves. No longer an option, I now had to face these feelings and learn how to deal with them. Life on life's terms.

I turned on the radio and sang at the top of my voice even though I wasn't feeling full of excitement at the prospect of heading back to a fresh start with Anna. Fake it to make it – another of AA's little truisms came into my head.

CHAPTER 24

My spirits sank when I walked into the silent house. It felt cold and there were no lights on in any of the rooms. I had secretly hoped for a welcome as heartfelt as the farewell I'd been given a couple of hours previously.

I dragged my bag inside and made a performance of shutting the door. Still nothing. I shouted at the top of my voice, "Hello?"

"Yes, yes, I'll be down in a minute!" came Anna's annoyed squawk from up in her office.

I flipped through the post on the kitchen table and found several cards addressed to me. Taking them into my office to open them, I made sure my new plant took pride of place on my desk. The cards were from friends wishing me all the best on this latest stage of my life journey. I walked back into the sitting room and was lining the cards up on the mantelpiece when Anna walked in.

"I can see you're back and making yourself at home. Move this bag out of the way, will you? It was amazing how much tidier the place was when you were away."

"Lovely to see you, too," I said in a non-combative way.

I gave her a hug before grabbing my offending suitcase, whisking it up to the spare room to unpack. I wasn't going to let her moods affect me any longer.

Back down stairs, I decided to get stuck into work. I'd suggested to Anna that we should sit down together so she could update me, but she shrugged and said there was nothing to report.

As I opened endless emails and scrolled through messages, it became obvious why there wasn't anything to report. Anna had done the square root of fuck all in my absence and there was some serious fire fighting ahead of me.

I felt pissed off about the poor-me act she had pulled at Lime House on family day. If she'd spent an hour on work over the past week, it was a generous assessment.

After several hours on the phone setting my business world to rights, I needed solace. An old bottle from my former life was waving at me from my desk drawer, but instead I went on-line to find an AA chat room. There were hundreds to choose from and it was reassuring to be able to communicate with a group of like-minded souls and find the support I needed instantly.

As the evening set in, I went upstairs to find Anna and see whether she had any specific plans for eating that night.

"Oh, not only am I supposed to have managed the business single-handedly, I am supposed to having done the shopping too?"

"What do you fancy eating and I'll pop down to the shop now?" I responded calmly although my insides were churning like a washing machine filled with despair.

"No, don't bother, there are some of those ready meals from Lidl in the freezer. We'll make do with them."

"I'll go and put them on then," I said, maintaining a cheerful façade.

"Don't put them in the oven and make another mess. Use the microwave."

I located the unappetising items Anna had suggested and heated them up, as directed, going outside for a cigarette whilst they cooked.

As I smoked, I imagined everyone at Lime House standing on the front doorstep at that very moment, sharing a joke whilst they convivially puffed away.

The ping of the microwave drew me back into the kitchen. Anna came downstairs, took one look at the sorry offering and decided she didn't want it after all. Opening my meal in a fit of pique, the boiling sauce spilt down my arm and leg before landing on the kitchen floor. I shouted out in pain.

"Treatment didn't help with your clumsiness, then?" Anna commented as she rolled her eyes heavenwards.

Having held my arm under the cold tap for several minutes and then changed my clothes, I was no longer in the mood to eat either. Anna was furious that I had wasted food and I could see she was going into one of her silent sulks, which often lasted for days.

"I'm going to start going to AA meetings tomorrow," I announced.

"Great. No sooner do you get back than you're off again. How long is this going to go on for?"

"For a lifetime," I answered smugly. "I've found someone to be my sponsor and she's going to take me to some different meetings over the next couple of weeks so I can find the ones I like the best."

"What's this woman's name and how old is she? Is she married?"

Anna bombarded me with questions, but I knew it wasn't out of interest. She was assessing whether my sponsor was a threat to her.

"Oh, for goodness sake. I don't know anything about the bloody woman. I've only spoken to her on the phone briefly. Why don't you come with me tomorrow if you're that worried?" I joked.

"I think I probably will," Anna replied and then turned her full attention to *Emmerdale*.

I fetched my laptop and sat down next to her. However, from all her huffing and puffing plus the black looks she was throwing my way,

I gathered she was not best pleased. I decided to go and sit in the kitchen to do some work as I was still playing catch-up from the previous week.

As I opened up my diary, it hit me that the Easter holidays were only a few weeks away and I hadn't sorted out anywhere to stay with the kids. I began trawling the internet and after a while, found a lovely barn conversion just a few miles from Anna's. I quickly fired off an email to check its availability and a response came whizzing straight back. Fortunately for me, they'd just had a cancellation and it was free for the very two weeks I needed.

Before I had a chance to get on with any work, Anna stormed in and stood next to me with her hands on her hips.

"I hope this new you isn't going to continue to be this cocky. What are you doing in here, for goodness sake? Work stops at five-thirty p.m., remember?"

"I was finding somewhere to stay with the kids at Easter. I'm sure you don't want them here for two weeks, do you?"

"Damn right I don't, especially your moody little daughter. Well, if you've finished doing that, you can come through and spend some time with me. *Coronation Street* is about to begin."

"I don't want to watch it," I said politely.

"Are you deliberately looking for an argument? I'll expect to see you in there soon."

She marched out, banging the door behind her.

I took a few deep breaths and tried to establish how I was feeling. Despite this on-going altercation with Anna, I realised I had no overwhelming desire to drink at all. It was a bloody miracle. And whilst I didn't want to get into an argument with her, I wasn't prepared to subjugate myself and go along with her demands either.

Had she always been this difficult? Was it simply because my mind had been constantly befuddled by booze that I'd been unable to see it before? Or was she feeling more insecure than ever and just acting up? Either way, I couldn't wait to get away again and spend a couple of weeks with the kids. It would also give me the chance to have a serious think about things.

I decided to go to bed early and read for a bit. I'd got into the habit of reading before going to sleep whilst at Lime House and really enjoyed it. It had been such a long time since I'd been able to concentrate on a good book.

As I made my way upstairs, I popped my head around the sitting room door to tell Anna I was off to bed. She muttered something but I didn't stop to find out what it was.

After a while, I turned out the lights and was soon fast asleep. The next thing I knew was the duvet being whipped off me by Anna, whilst shouting at the top of her voice. I could tell by her slurred speech that she'd been drinking. I wasn't going to get into a fight and provide her with another opportunity to call the police. Pulling the duvet back around me, I ignored her and pretended to go back to sleep.

She then got into bed herself and began pushing and kicking me, making it obvious she wanted me out. I was more than happy to oblige and made a dash for the spare room. I quickly created a makeshift lock for the door by moving the bedside table against it and wedging a pile of books under the door handle.

Anna tried to force her way in, banging and shouting on the other side of the door. I held a pillow over my head and repeated the Serenity Prayer again and again in my head as if I were counting celestial sheep. It seemed to do the trick and I dozed off, leaving Anna making a scene on the other side of the door. Shame she didn't have an audience to appreciate her performance. God knows how long she was out there.

When I woke the next morning, I felt elated. I could remember everything that had gone on the night before and knew I was entirely blameless. It was a fantastic feeling to have a completely clear head, absolutely no trace of a hangover and be able to begin my day without a round of apologies to make. I also knew that I'd pretty much have the day to myself. After the amount of alcohol Anna had obviously consumed, I imagined she'd be confined to bed with a blinding migraine for most of it.

CHAPTER 25

Despite feeling and looking like macerated shit, Anna was as good as her word and managed to haul herself along to my first AA meeting that evening to meet Deidre, my sponsor.

As it turned out Deidre was a widow, stood just under five feet tall, and had the presence of a church mouse. The meeting itself featured the usual cross section of humanity that I'd come to expect.

Anna decided she had nothing to worry about and never came to any of my meetings again. She did, however, continue to resent the fact I spent two nights a week at AA and usually ignored me for the rest of the evening when I got home.

Her behaviour went from bad to worse. She tried picking arguments with me at every opportunity and leapfrogged from one criticism to the next. Maybe it had always been this way and I'd just never been sober enough to notice.

When I didn't react or rise to the argument, she got angrier still, shouting abuse at me and goading me like a spiteful child with a particularly sharp stick.

Whenever Anna started having a go, I'd imagine myself back at Lime House or fantasise about what I'd do with the kids this Easter. It was the mental equivalent of putting my fingers in my ears and going 'lalalalalala' whilst she continued to rant in the background like rather unpleasant lift music.

I began writing lists and packing my clothes a week in advance of the Easter break. A few days before I was due to pick up the kids, Anna's mood swung in the opposite direction like a breeze spinning a weather vane from north to south. Maybe it was some Pavlovian response to seeing me with my suitcases and getting ready to leave.

Despite her mood change, I still found myself doing everything solo when it came to the kids. She always devolved herself of any responsibility by reminding me they were "not her children."

As I set off to fetch them, I was overcome with relief. Anna, on the other hand, had tears in her eyes as she waved goodbye to me from the window.

When we arrived at the barn, the kids were thrilled with it. It was massive and there was so much space inside, they could run around without fear of knocking anything over. It came complete with table football and a swing attached to a beam. Compared to some of the places we'd shacked up in recent years, it was truly palatial.

Outside in the surrounding fields there were chickens, sheep, a small fishing lake and a huge trampoline to keep them occupied. I was equally as taken with the place. My bedroom had a back door opening out onto stone steps that led down to a field – the perfect smoking retreat.

As I sat out there on the first night, with the kids already tucked up in bed, I gazed at the stars and realised how comfortable I felt being there alone. Life just kept getting better.

The four of us got into a routine. Each morning, we'd walk along the bridleway, which wound its way up to a wooded hilltop - the perfect way to create an appetite for our daily breakfast of boiled eggs and soldiers.

I did as much work as I could from the barn although, without internet access, I had to go back to Anna's from time to time. She put in an appearance at the barn once in a while. Usually whenever we were off for a meal or doing something that took her fancy. When she stayed over, I ignored her demands for tea and toast in bed in the morning. I also insisted we watch something everyone would enjoy in the evening rather than succumbing to her demands to watch the soaps. All this in spite of her pouting.

A couple of days before Good Friday, I got a call from a potential client inviting me to take part in a pitch for a fairly sizeable piece of new business. It would mean being away for the day as they were based in the south. I couldn't very well drag the kids all the way down there so I asked Anna if she would come over and babysit for the day. She refused.

I didn't waste any time trying to persuade her. Instead, I made arrangements with the woman who owned the barn and lived right next door. She had kids herself and understood the problems of trying to juggle family life and a job. She agreed to keep an eye on them and make sure that they were fine. I gave her Anna's contact details in case of an emergency.

Anna grudgingly committed to popping over at lunchtime to make sure the kids ate something decent.

My trip was a complete success from a business perspective, but when I got home, I was dismayed to find the barn had taken on the appearance of an overturned skip. There were empty Coke cans, crisp packets and sweet wrappers scattered everywhere. Half-eaten Jammie Dodgers were ground into the carpet and chocolatey fingerprints were in evidence all over the whitewashed walls. Fortunately, my children were all alive and well.

As luck would have it, my neighbour's elderly mother had died suddenly. Apparently, the neighbour had left a message with Anna to explain what had happened and asking her to come over for the day.

Anna had not only reneged on her lunchtime promise, she also hadn't put in an appearance at any stage of the day. I tortured myself with thoughts about all the horrible accidents that could have befallen my three unattended offspring. I phoned Anna to give her a piece of my mind. I wasn't interested in hearing her excuses or her whining and after delivering my speech, put the phone down on her.

Packing the children into the car, I drove to Anna's favourite restaurant for a three-course meal. Anna was furious when she found out where we'd been. She was so proprietorial about the place but I was buggered if I was going to invite her along.

I managed to put a lid on my anger in time for Easter Day itself. I'd invited my parents to come over for lunch. Anna had suggested Arthur should join us as he was going to be on his own and I'd asked Deidre along too.

As per usual, Anna turned up too late to help with any of the preparations or even to lay the table. Arthur and Anna were so engrossed in conversation at the end of the meal, they were the only two who didn't lend a hand with any of the washing-up. Even the kids pitched in!

Yet again I found myself asking whether she had always been this lazy and uncaring? What the fuck was I doing with her? I was so angry, I realised I'd wound a tea towel around my hand whilst having these uncharitable thoughts to the point I'd almost cut off my circulation.

In the afternoon I organised an Easter Egg hunt outside in the garden for the kids. After everyone else had left, Anna had a mood because I had not included her in the Easter Egg hunt. She thought I'd been very unfair knowing how much she liked chocolate.

In the past I would have felt guilty, apologised and done my utmost to make things up to her. God, how pathetic I had been. Well, not anymore. I couldn't believe what I was hearing. I told her to listen to herself, to stop being childish and to 'fucking' grow up. I knew that this would result in her driving off in a huff – in fact that had been my intention. I just wanted a quiet evening with the kids.

During the second week of the Easter break, I spent as much time as I could with my children. We went to the cinema, cooked and baked endless cakes, went on picnics and visited stately homes and castles. I felt gutted when it was time to hand them over to MDH as I was going to miss them dreadfully.

MDH and I decided to split the journey and meet halfway. On the spur of the moment, we agreed to all have lunch together. I found myself enjoying MDH's company for the first time in years. I apologised to him for my part in our marriage breakdown as well as for all the drunken episodes he'd had to put up with.

"Would you like us to give it another go?" he asked.

"No, we're not right for each other, apart from the obvious complication of my being gay," I said in hushed tones, trying to make light of the situation.

I felt awful extinguishing his final flame of hope and something in his eyes seemed to fade. Anna might have been a mistake, but I knew I would never go back to being straight. Had I still been drinking, I might well have agreed to a reunion with MDH. Alcohol made me weak and my 'any bottle of port in a storm' philosophy had served me well in the past.

After saying our goodbyes, I sat in the car park for at least half an hour after MDH had driven off with the kids. With reluctance, I started my engine and headed north. Back to Anna.

Before going 'home', I needed to collect everything from the barn. By the time I had packed up and tidied the place, it was getting late. Not quite ready to let go of my happy Easter memories, I decided to stay the night there instead of making the ten-minute drive back to

Anna's. I sent her a text informing her of my plan. She responded with several choice texts of her own just as I'd expected.

It was that night I decided I had no choice other than to leave Anna. I knew if I stayed with her, I might very well start drinking again at some stage in the future. I felt wretched. She was the first person I had truly loved. Despite knowing there was something not quite right about her, I still had feelings for her .

But for the first time in my life, I felt strong enough to make it on my own. In the past, whenever I'd broken up with someone, I'd always made sure I had another pair of arms to run to. This time I knew it wasn't about replacing Anna with someone else. How could I when I still cared so deeply?

This was about making the right decision for my wellbeing. Without that, I'd be good for nothing and no one. The time had come for me to move on. I was growing up at last.

CHAPTER 26

Leaving Anna wasn't going to be straightforward, like breaking up with anyone 'normal', I knew that much. There was no way we could simply sit down, have a heart-to-heart and, after a few bitter recriminations, divide up our CD collection.

If I'd so much as hinted I was off, she'd have probably stripped me naked and chained me up in the garage. I knew she would do anything in her power to ensure I stayed with her.

I decided a month should be long enough to sort everything out. I'd have to play my cards close to my chest to avoid raising the slightest suspicion. This meant I was going to have to plan my departure with military precision. Perhaps my time with MDH was about to pay off.

The decision to move back to the Cotswolds to be closer to the kids was a no-brainer. I'd always seemed more at peace in that part of the world and it was the only place where I felt I belonged.

An email was sent to my parents informing them of my grand plan and then instantly deleted to avoid prying eyes. Needless to say, they were delighted by my decision and fell over themselves to assist in the conspiracy.

My mum offered to contact all the local estate agents and get together a list of places to rent.

My dad and I organised a couple of dates to rendezvous on the A1. I was to pack my car with as many of my things as possible to hand over to him. He would then take them back and store them for the time being.

Although I knew it was the right thing to do, my heart ached for Anna. It seemed cruel to continue living our life together as if everything was ginger peachy whilst I was preparing a bid for freedom behind her back. She remained oblivious to my little scheme, which made it harder still.

I registered a new company name and bought the website domain. I also spoke to the bank and arranged for a new business account to be set up.

Getting across to the Cotswolds to view the properties proved straightforward. I pretended there was a potential client in the area who wanted to meet. Anna knew my mother didn't particularly like her so showed no desire to accompany me on the trip if it involved the possibility of 'seeing the dragon'.

As I toured an assortment of dismal little flats in the centre of one town, my heart sank. I hadn't lived anywhere so basic since my student days. How would I be able to cope with the kids through the holidays in somewhere so small?

The last property was a cottage in an area I didn't know that well. It proved really hard to find but eventually after venturing down a tiny path, I discovered it behind a huge wooden gate.

Surely there'd been a mistake? It was like walking into *The Secret Garden*. A picture book cottage stood in front of me surrounded on all four sides by a pretty little garden. Although it was in the middle of other houses, it was completely secluded – my own private oasis. How on earth could this be within my price range, I wondered?

Having been shown round by the estate agent, I was in love with the place and agreed to take it immediately. All they needed to do was make a few background checks and, within the month, I'd be able to move in. I felt so excited, I almost called Anna to tell her the good news before I realised that was not the smartest of ideas.

Talking of Anna, she seemed to be spending less and less time working on the business if that were humanly possible. She was always finding excuses to be out shopping or visiting car showrooms in the area. She seemed to change her vehicles more often than her girlfriends. In the time I'd known her, she had already been through three of them (cars, not girlfriends).

It was the first time I was relieved about her lack of commitment to work. It provided me with the time I needed to secretly stow things in my car. I became a dab hand at locating previously unknown storage spaces. Perhaps a future in drug smuggling lay ahead of me?

The time arrived for my first get-together with my old dad. We kept it reasonably brief. I didn't want to have to come up with some convoluted story as to why I was handing endless overstuffed bin liners to an elderly man in a lay-by. It would have been just my luck to be spotted by a local and the news to get back to Anna. I was still horribly aware of owning the title 'village drunk', so I didn't need further strange goings on fanning the flames of my legacy.

In the meantime, Anna's campaign to drive me back to drink gathered pace. During a lengthy monologue of moaning, she confessed that she preferred me when I was drinking.

"Why don't you think about taking it up again?" she suggested, as if she was talking about knitting.

I ignored her and continued working, pretending to be completely absorbed in what I was doing.

"You were more loving and attentive before you went into treatment," she continued.

Needy and desperate, more like. She seemed to be panicking about her loss of control over me. I no longer got involved in any bickering and neither did I jump to attention when she asked me to do something or stop doing something.

When she was at home, Anna started spending more time working downstairs with me in the conservatory. Barely did a phone call go by without her muttering away in the background or throwing in a grenade of a remark or two. I learnt to ignore her, just as I had done the intrusive sound of planes coming in to land when we'd lived right under the main Heathrow flight path.

This only irritated her further and she would goad me with insults, which got increasingly unpleasant as time went on. I decided to keep a log of everything she said or did. Knowing myself as I was beginning to, a time was bound to come when I would romanticise what life had been like with Anna. It would be good to remind myself how awful things had been and shock some sense into me.

As Anna continued to berate me, I continued to sneak my belongings out to the car. Eventually my possessions were down to a bare minimum and I was amazed Anna hadn't noticed anything amiss. My life with Anna was now little more than the façade of a few theatrical props.

After the final secret get-together with my father, all that was left for me to pack were the things from the office, my jewellery, some toiletries and a couple of big items, which were just too obvious to move in advance.

Anna had booked to have her eyebrows re-tattooed one Friday. I knew the woman who specialised in this permanent make-up technique was based at least fifty miles away. The procedure took a good hour or so and, as Anna was also planning to have some other facial rearrangements, she'd be gone for hours. Here was my window of opportunity to get the hell out of Dodge.

Two days before Departure Day, Anna announced that she wanted to take me out for a romantic meal. She'd already booked a table for Thursday evening at a restaurant she knew I wanted to try. Her treat. You could have knocked me down with a feather. Had she discovered my plan?

After thinking it through, knowing Anna, if she had found out I was on the verge of doing a runner, spoiling me with a night out would not have been her style. No, this was just one of those awful cases of truly crap timing.

Thursday arrived and I knew, for my on-going sanity and wellbeing, I had to go through with my plan the following day. It was no way to live: bickering, game-playing and trying to outmanoeuvre each other.

Now that I knew what life could be like without being dependent on drink, I needed to deal with all my other addictions. And Anna was just that. How else could I explain the desire to stay with someone who wanted to destroy everything about me?

That didn't mean I had stopped caring about her. I still found her sexy and desirable and, when things were good between us, the world took on a magical quality. But when it was bad, it was beyond horrid. The 'magical' moments were so few and far between these days. This was mainly because I refused to go along with everything Anna demanded.

So it was with a heavy heart I got ready for our night out. To make matters worse, Anna looked bloody gorgeous.

"Lovely Anna," I said remorsefully, stroking her cheek.

"You're the lovely one," she responded, kissing me gently.

"Neither of us are truly lovely," I sighed.

The words came spilling out and I knew the moment they'd escaped, I had said the wrong thing. Anna's face hardened and her body language changed. She muttered 'charming' before getting into the car.

We drove in silence to the restaurant, but Anna's mood shifted back more quickly than usual and she reached for my hand, smiling. What the buggery bollocks was going on? I prayed for the strength to stick to my decision. I didn't want to go back to being a compliant puppy who, with one kind word from its cruel master, would roll around playfully on its back before being on the receiving end of another good kicking.

We chatted amiably and Anna got quite tipsy on several glasses of wine. The food was fantastic and the irony of the Last Supper was not lost on me, although I couldn't decide whether I should cast myself as Jesus or Judas.

When we got home, Anna led me up to the bedroom and tried to undress me. I couldn't be doing with it. I pushed her away, turned my back on her and mumbled something clichéd about "having a headache." Thankfully Anna soon fell asleep. As she lay there curled up foetally, I gazed at her. She always looked so vulnerable when she was sleeping. Everything about her physical appearance was delicate, like fine bone china.

Despite having been taken aback by her looks when we first met, I now found her extraordinarily attractive. How long would it take I wondered, to stop feeling like this and not find myself tied in knots?

I knew it was time for me to start behaving as a responsible adult. I had to get past this teenage crush phase of my life. Anna wanted to live in a bubble with just the two of us inside it. She didn't want to be bothered with the realities of life or anything that went on in the real world.

It was time to pop the bubble.

CHAPTER 28

Departure Day arrived. To me, it seemed such a momentous occasion that I half expected ominous, *GhostBuster*-style clouds to be thundering across the skies accompanied by a dramatic theme tune. But it was just another ordinary day. Grey skies the colour of washed-out undies, co-ordinated perfectly with my washing line of wrung-out emotions. Instead of the orchestra, the sound of breakfast telly filled the bedroom.

Anna was up and about early getting ready for her appointment with the tattooist. It irked me how much more commitment she had to personal grooming than she'd ever had to the business. I used these stirrings of anger to stoke up my commitment to the day that lay ahead of me.

I got up, made some very strong coffee and went out onto the decking for a cigarette. I prefixed everything with 'this is the last time I shall' in a further bid to bolster my resolve.

It remained critical to continue with my charade and not alert Anna that something was amiss. I went into the office and started up my laptop. Several emails appeared in my in-box from those in the know wishing me all the best. Even my best friend, who never normally had a bad word to say about anyone, had never got on with Anna. She sensed she was 'heartless'. I deleted all the evidence as soon as I'd read them.

I hadn't even written my letter of goodbye to Anna just in case she had happened upon it in advance. I had been so careful to cover all my tracks.

I emailed the bank instructing them to prohibit Anna from withdrawing any further money from the business account or from using her company card. There was about ten thousand pounds in there at the moment. We'd have to discuss how to split it, but that could wait for a few weeks until things had settled down.

I also needed to speak to the utility companies and put a stop to all the blasted direct debits Anna had set up. I decided to grab the chance to make these calls whilst Anna was upstairs showering.

Having dealt with the electricity, I was on the phone to the gas provider. As I was finishing the call hunched in my chair with my back to the door, I felt the hair on the back of my neck prickling. I wasn't alone.

In disbelief I turned around to find Anna leaning on the doorframe, arms crossed and an expression of hate on her face that even I had not witnessed previously. She was topless, having got half undressed for her shower before popping downstairs to feed Bugsy.

"Bitch!" she spat at me. "Bitch, bitch, bitch!"

At that point, she hadn't grasped the full significance of my actions. She had taken them at face value and assumed I was transferring the direct debits back into her account as a single act of revenge. Fortunately for me, her instinct was to dash upstairs to her office and call back the utility companies.

I knew this was my only chance. I had to make a dash for it there and then. There was no time to collect any more of my stuff or write my 'Dear John' letter. Once she grasped the reality of what was happening, I dreaded to think what she'd be capable of doing.

I grabbed my laptop, my little Lime House plant, my mobile, the car keys and a couple of treasured knick-knacks from my desk.

Adrenalin pumped through me and my heart felt like it was going to burst through my chest. I ran out to my car. The front door slammed behind me and must have caught Anna's attention. As I started the engine and began backing out of the drive, she appeared, still topless, sneering and gesticulating like a crazed she-devil. She tried opening the various car doors but I'd made certain to auto-lock them as soon as I'd got in.

She threw herself on the bonnet of the car grabbing the windscreen wipers. One of them bent and the only thing I could think of in that moment was how much it looked like one of the TeleTubbies' antennas.

I continued reversing and Anna was forced to let go of the wipers. Making a swift U-turn and just managing not to hit her, I thrust the car into gear and headed into the village. She ran down the road after me. I looked in my rear-view mirror to see her screaming obscenities at me. Then her half-naked torso disappeared into the distance. Another 'only gay in the village' story for the locals to dine out on.

My chest felt tight – it all seemed so unreal. After a couple of miles, I pulled into a garage car park in an attempt to calm down. My hands were shaking and my heart was still going ten to the dozen. I must have smoked an entire pack of cigarettes in the space of an hour and the inside of the car took on all the appeal of a kipper factory. I still had all the doors locked and didn't want to open any of the windows just in case Anna put in a stealth attack.

Should I forget about the things I'd left at her house? As I continued to contemplate my next move, the mobile rang. I assumed it was Anna and didn't answer it. When I played back the message, I discovered it was the bank. Anna had transferred the ten thousand pounds from the business into her personal account five minutes ago. I'd forgotten to instruct them to block the on-line banking facility. Bollocks. I doubted I'd ever see a penny of that money again but it made me more determined not to leave her with a single possession of mine. Especially my jewellery, which included a charm bracelet my godmother had left to me in her will.

I decided to call the police, explain my situation and ask them to accompany me whilst I retrieved my belongings.

They told me they'd be there within the hour. Still furious with myself about the on-line banking fuck up, I knocked back several soft drinks as I would have a six-pack of lager only a few months before.

Driving back to Anna's felt wrong, almost as if I'd failed. I parked several hundred yards down the road from her house, making sure I was out of view, and waited for the police to arrive.

When they turned up, one of them wandered over to my car for a briefing. We recognised each other immediately. He was the very same policeman who had arrested me that night I'd ended up in Melton Mowbray police station. This time he was charming, almost apologetic. He suggested I stayed in my car whilst they went to have a word with Anna in the first instance.

He returned a few minutes later. She was refusing to let them accompany me into the house, but she was happy for me to go in alone. No surprises there then. It was at that point, the policeman I knew said:

"We don't think you should go in alone though. She's unstable."

"What should I do?"

"We'll pull into the drive, you follow us and park behind our car but don't get out and keep all your doors locked."

Now they were scaring me.

"Do you think she'll try something then?"

"She's put you behind bars once and is now refusing the police access to her house. That's not the way normal people carry on. But if she sees you, she might change her mind about allowing us in to collect your things."

The words 'not normal' resonated with a strange familiarity.

I followed the police car into the drive as instructed. As they were getting out, Anna appeared at the front door, her eye make-up streaked from crying. Obviously her tears hadn't blinded her sufficiently to stop performing on-line banking transactions. Crocodile tears, maybe? I was unsure these days how much of Anna was genuine or whether most of it was fake.

On spotting me, she ran over and tried to force her arm through my slightly open driver's window. She flailed about, trying to reach for the key in the engine. It took both policemen to restrain her.

"That's my car she's driving!" she shouted. "Give me the keys!"

"I pay for the car but it *is* registered in her name," I admitted to the policemen.

"It's still stealing!" she hissed.

"As is taking ten thousand pounds out of the business account," I added.

Anna just sneered at me, still fighting to free herself from the policemen's grasp. The one I knew approached my car again as the other one held her back, struggling to keep a grip on her.

The policeman indicated to me to wind my window down and leaned in to have a quiet word.

"Even if she decided to report the car as stolen, it won't be picked up immediately. My advice to you is forget your stuff and get out of here now."

"Can't I go in whilst you keep her out here?"

"'Fraid not – besides, it's not worth it love. She's not right in the head, she really isn't. You want to get away while you can."

His words knocked me for six yet again. I'd been living with this woman for a year. How could she not be "right in the head?"

I started my car and watched the realisation dawn on Anna's face that I was leaving for good this time. I wasn't going to ignore sound advice from other people and run back into her arms. I no longer believed I was the chosen one or that I had the power to change Anna.

She began screaming again, referring to the policemen as fucking cunts – a tried-and-tested method for endearing yourself to officers of the law. She continued wrestling with them, desperately trying to free herself from their hold. Her face was contorted with anger and the last mental snapshot I have of her was her crumpled red grimace as I rounded the corner.

Speeding through the lanes, the countryside seemed vividly in focus. It was almost as if my brain was taking its final visual inventory of a place that had been important to me for a small part of my life. Almost home but not quite.

There was the village green and the phone box, which had the dubious status of being the landmarks commemorating my personal rock bottom. I passed the shop and an assortment of inns and watering holes all of which I had staggered into and out of in various states of inebriation.

Sitting at the edge of memory lane was the very restaurant we'd eaten at last night. One of the few meals Anna had paid for. That had really rankled with her and was one of the last insults she had lobbed my way as I left. Can't say I blame her.

Too numb to feel anything much or shed a tear, I concentrated on my driving and putting enough miles between Anna and myself to feel

I'd reached neutral territory. As I'd anticipated, my phone soon sprang into a frenzy of action.

The police had obviously moved on as Anna had begun her incessant texting. I could predict exactly the pattern they would follow. The initial ones would be abusive before they mellowed into pleas for my return followed by saccharin sweet expressions of love.

When it finally rang, I decided to answer. I'd not been able to explain in writing to Anna why I had decided to leave her once and for all. Surely I owed her that one last courtesy?

Her voice sounded paper thin on the other end of the phone and all I could make out was her sobbing. Then her familiar reprise began.

No one would ever love me like she did. She had never felt so deeply about anyone. I was her soul mate. She didn't think she would be able to live without me. I was the best thing that had ever happened to her. She'd never been so happy.

I let her drone on until she had exhausted her entire arsenal.

"It's over, Anna."

She began to wail down the phone but I ignored her and continued with my spiel.

"We're no good together. We're in a competition not a relationship and over the last few months, things have got out of hand. You resent the fact I've given up drinking. I cannot live in this turmoil any more and stay sober."

I could tell Anna was desperate to cut across me but I carried on.

"I also want to make sure my kids have a proper home. Given you find it impossible to be around them for any length of time, that's never going to happen if we stay together."

Anna just repeated the word 'no' over and over again.

"There isn't anyone else, I promise you that. But I am tired out trying to change things. We cannot even have a rational conversation – you never admit to being wrong."

Even in the height of this crisis, with the infrastructure of her life crashing down around her, Anna was unable to put forward an adult response. She became predictably defensive.

"Everyone thinks your kids are hard work, sweetheart. If you loved me, you'd come back here right now, you really are a funny…"

Her words morphed into noises and I stopped listening. I pressed the red button on my phone and laid it on the seat beside me.

From narrow country lanes to the faster A roads and finally onto the motorway, it felt good knowing Anna would soon be hundreds of miles away. I even started to feel a twinge of excitement at the possibilities life now promised.

I'd be able to join a gym and start exercising again. I could eat healthy food without being told I was obsessed with my weight. I'd be able to see my kids whenever I liked, just like a real mum. No more hours glued to the TV watching the soaps – I could start going to the cinema or take up an evening class.

As I mentally scrolled through all my options, I became intensely aware of all the restrictions Anna had placed upon me. And I had been a willing victim. It had happened over such a long period of time, it had been insidious.

I was free. I had left MDH for Anna believing her to be my saviour. I had been deluded. Now I had left Anna – for myself.

My little cottage was waiting for me and I could continue my journey to adulthood. At that moment my phone beeped. Yet another text from Anna.

This time I didn't read it or bother replying to it. I simply deleted it.

"You go, girl, and don't you go back," I said to myself.

I felt a smile spread across my face as I put my foot on the accelerator and moved out into the fast lane.